THE SURGEON'S MIRACLE BABY

BY
CAROL MARINELLI

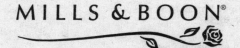

MILLS & BOON®

First published in Great Britain 2006
Paperback edition 2007
Harlequin Mills & Boon Limited,
Eton House, 18-24 Paradise Road, Richmond, Surrey TW9 1SR

© Carol Marinelli 2006

ISBN-13: 978 0 263 85212 7
ISBN-10:   0 263 85212 1

Set in Times Roman 10½ on 13 pt
03-0107-50255

Printed and bound in Spain
by Litografia Rosés, S.A., Barcelona

THE SURGEON'S
MIRACLE BABY

PROLOGUE

'HE'LL be OK at the crèche, won't he?' Louise stared into the carry seat at her sleeping son, watching as a gummy smile flickered over Declan's face, his eyelids flickering as he dreamed milky dreams, utterly oblivious to the hellish guilt that was racking his overwrought mother.

'He'll be fine,' Maggie groaned, snuggling into her dressing-gown and nursing a large mug of tea as she stood in the hallway of the tiny third-floor flat they were sharing. 'It's his mother I'm more worried about. You'll end up in my ward with me taking care of you if you don't lose some of the guilt!'

Which was surely a joke, but given that Maggie was a psychiatric nurse, it wasn't in the best of taste!

'It's normal to be anxious on the first day in a new job,' Louise said defensively. 'And it's my first day back at work since I had him—I'm still breast-feeding, remember.'

'As if I could forget! I heard that blessed breast pump going all night—you've got enough milk in that cool bag to feed the whole crèche.' Maggie's joking façade faded as she saw the anguish on her friend's face.

'He'll be fine,' she said gently, putting down her mug on

the hall table and pulling Louise into a hug. 'He's going to be ten minutes down the corridor from you, being loved and fussed over in the hospital crèche while his mummy's earning lots of lovely money.'

'I know.' Louise sniffed. 'To tell the truth, it's not just Declan I'm worried about—I feel as if I've forgotten everything I know.'

'It'll all come back the second you set foot on the ward.'

'Do you really think so?' Louise asked dubiously.

'I promise,' Maggie said assuredly. 'And at the end of the day you're a casual nurse—they're hardly going to be expecting you to run the show and you can just ease yourself in gently. Remember, a little more than a year ago you were a senior RN on a high-dependency unit in one of London's busiest hospitals. Childbirth can't have scrambled your brains that much!'

'Were you nervous?' Louise asked. 'I mean, when you came here to Melbourne and had to start all over again?'

'No,' Maggie answered, then laughed. 'But I'm a psychiatric nurse, remember! People are the same whatever side of the globe you're on. Go!' she said, picking up the car seat and handing it over to Louise. 'Do you want a hand to get down the stairs?'

'No, thanks.' Louise shook her head but after bypassing the out-of-order lift and struggling down the stairwell with car seat, nappy bag, handbag and baby, she wished she hadn't been quite so proud! Strapping Declan into the back of the car, Louise climbed into the driver's seat, flicked on her lights and glanced at the clock on the dashboard, guilt layered on guilt as she saw that it was only six-thirty in the morning and that she'd dragged her sleeping babe up. She was so grateful to Maggie for being there.

Mad Maggie! They'd met a couple of years back on the other side of the world. Louise had been starting out on the adventure of a lifetime—a working holiday in the UK. She had been working a night shift in a busy London teaching hospital and Maggie had been on the surgical ward, specialling a psychiatric patient who had attempted suicide. Chatting, as night nurses invariably did, they'd hit it off immediately.

Both adored shoes but hated pedicures.

Both had credit limits on their cards that would make most mortals faint with shock.

And both were holding out for Mr Perfect.

'Mr *Really* Perfect,' Louise had elaborated, peeling open a box of chicken snacks at some ungodly hour and hoping that the carbohydrate rush would see her through to the morning. 'Someone who will still make my knees knock when I'm fifty.'

'Someone rich,' Maggie had sighed, 'someone who can afford my liposuction and Botox when *I'm* fifty!'

It had turned out that Maggie had been looking for a new flatmate and Louise had fitted the bill.

How times had changed.

Nearly two years later, it was Maggie now on a working holiday.

Maggie who had landed in Melbourne and had borrowed Louise's spare room in her small rented flat for a few nights, which had turned into a few weeks!

And it was Maggie waving her off as she stepped out into the world on her first day as a working, single mother.

CHAPTER ONE

'SORRY, what was your surname again?'

'Andrews,' Louise repeated, her bag over her shoulder, standing awkwardly as everyone else sat and trying not to blush as a very pretty but clearly irritated nurse relayed her details down the telephone to the nursing co-ordinator in front of the entire handover room. She was already feeling self-conscious enough in her new navy uniform, with new navy shoes and newly trimmed long dark wavy hair tied back with a new navy hair tie and now, and to make her feel even more self-conscious, the charge nurse seemed far from pleased to see her.

'Hi, Kelly, it's Elaine here on ASU. I've got a Louise Andrews here from the hospital bank—she says that she's booked to work here for the next four weeks to cover Del's sick leave, but Del was rostered for a late shift today.' The longest pause ensued, the night staff yawning loudly, no doubt keen to get handover out of the way so they could head for home, while, in contrast, the day staff chatted happily, sipping their coffee and catching up on news—clearly in no particular rush to get out on the ward and start working.

'How can she possibly be down for four weeks of early

shifts?' Elaine's surprised voice snapped everyone to attention. 'Since when did Del only work early shifts? If the bank nurse is supposed to be covering for Del, surely she should just take over her roster.'

Another horribly long pause ensued, only this time it wasn't filled with idle chatter—and Louise could feel every eye on her as Elaine's far from dulcet tones filled the room.

'Oh, we'd all *love* to pick and choose when we work, Kelly, but for most of us it isn't possible! Now it would seem that I'm going to have to spend the best part of the morning changing my regular staff's shifts to accommodate a *casual*. It's simply not on. Either Sister Adams—I mean Andrews— is to come back at one p.m. for the late shift or another nurse will need to be arranged to cover Del's roster.'

A year ago she'd have been tempted to turn tail and run— correction, Louise thought, a year ago she would have crumbled on the uncomfortable spot and offered to work each and every one of the mysterious Del's shifts and anything else in between just to get this difficult moment over with—but a lot of things had changed since a year ago, so instead Louise stood if not firm then feebly resolute, pointedly not saying anything until, with a very pained sigh, Elaine handed her the telephone.

'The nursing co-ordinator wants to talk to you. Could you take it outside, please, so that we can get on with handover?'

Which meant one of two things. Either she was about to spend the entire morning barely knowing what was going on with the patients, thanks to missing out on handover, or— Louise gulped at the least palatable option—she was going home.

Without a word and with an incredibly steady hand, given the circumstances, Louise took the phone and headed out into the corridor, making sure the door was closed behind her before speaking to the nursing co-ordinator. She was determined to keep calm, determined not to let the knot of anxiety that was in her stomach creep into her voice, but her eyes were screwed closed as Kelly introduced herself. Leaning against the wall, Louise waited to find out if the weeks of careful planning and major upheaval had all been worth it, waited to find out if she actually had a job.

'Is Elaine giving you a hard time?' A tinkle of laughter from the nursing co-ordinator had Louise peeling her eyes open. 'I'm Kelly, by the way.'

'Hi, Kelly,' Louise said, relieved to hear a friendly voice and warming to the other woman's tone. 'It would seem that Elaine wants me to take over Del's shifts; but I'm sorry—I'm just not able to. I did say at my interview that I could only work early shifts and only on weekdays—'

'Don't apologise,' Kelly cut in. 'The whole point of being a bank nurse is being able to choose your shifts. Elaine should be counting herself lucky that we've been able to send the ward an experienced surgical nurse. Did you tell her just how qualified you are?'

'We didn't actually get that far with introductions,' Louise admitted.

'Well, it was either you and four weeks of early shifts or a grad nurse straight out of uni—and if I were the one in charge of the acute surgical unit this morning, I know who I'd choose!'

'So it's OK for me to stay?'

'Absolutely. Look, you're going to have to grow a thick skin pretty fast, I'm afraid, Louise. The hospital bank is still fairly new—till a few months ago we used an agency. Some of our ward staff can't quite get used to the idea that a casual staff member should get to choose their shifts, get a better hourly rate of pay *and* use the facilities like the gym and crèche. Feel free to point out to them that your work isn't guaranteed, and there's no such thing as sick pay or annual leave…' Kelly was no doubt trying to help, but as she pointed out the pitfalls of being a bank nurse, Louise felt that familiar knot of anxiety tighten a fraction, the precariousness of her situation not something she wanted to dwell on right now. 'The fact of the matter is,' Kelly continued, 'it's far better for the hospital to have our own team of casual nurses—you get to know the wards, and we get to know you, so everyone wins.'

'Thanks for that,' Louise said, though she was sure that Elaine would take rather a lot more convincing, 'I'd better get back to handover.'

'Sure. Oh, and, Louise…' Just as she was about to ring off Kelly called her back. 'There's an eight-week stretch coming up in Outpatients, just after you finish on the surgical ward. The hours are eight till four, except on Wednesdays when you'd have to stay till five. The work might not be quite as varied or interesting as you're used to, but the hours are great and at least you'd know where you'd be for a while.'

'It sounds great,' Louise enthused. 'How do I apply?'

'You just have to say yes.' Kelly laughed. 'Can I put you down?'

'Sure.' Louise blinked. 'I mean, yes, please.'

'Done! I'll pop the details in your pigeonhole. Now, if you have any more problems with Elaine, just give me a call, but I'll be up on the ward doing my rounds around eleven. I'll come and say hello to you then. Welcome to Melbourne General!'

Even Elaine's sour expression as she walked back into the meeting room and took her seat at the table couldn't dampen her spirits.

Eight more weeks of guaranteed work!

OK, outpatients wasn't exactly cutting-edge nursing, but Louise truly didn't care. She'd have directed the traffic in the staff car park if it guaranteed her a wage! Eight weeks on top of these four meant that she had work for the next three months. It would see her right up through Christmas, and also meant she could start looking around for a rather more suitable home!

'We're up to bed nine.' The nurse next to her pushed a handover sheet towards her as the lethargic night nurse—who'd been yawning before—now zipped through the patients with renewed energy, clearly buoyed by the prospect of home and bed. 'I'll fill you in on the rest after handover. I'm Shona by the way.'

'Thanks, Shona.' Louise smiled, snapping on her pen and running her eyes down the handover sheet, which thankfully contained the names and details of all the patients on the ward with a space left for her to add her own notes. Despite the rocky start to the morning, despite the rather frozen look on Elaine's face as she'd returned and sat down, Louise was utterly determined to enjoy the rest of the day—back in the workforce, doing the job she loved. Nothing could spoil that except…

Room 3 Age 35 Danny Ashwood APFI

For a second Louise froze, reading again the small amount of information about the patient in Room 3 and trying desperately at the same time to concentrate on the details that were being given about the patient in Room 10.

It couldn't be him, Louise scolded herself, writing down a complicated antibiotic and IV regime, listening carefully to the handover. But at the same time a small part of her brain was having its own conversation and every now and then, between patients or when the handover was interrupted by a phone call or a nurse popping her head around the door for the drug key, Louise couldn't help but listen to the argument that was raging somewhere in her mind.

It couldn't be him because for one thing he lived in England! As if Daniel would be here in Melbourne.

As if!

Anyway, this patient was called Danny—Daniel never shortened his name! And it wasn't exactly a rare one—there must be loads of thirty-five-year-old Daniel Ashwoods around the world and no doubt a fair share of them were in hospital at this very moment with abdo pain for investigation.

It could even be a woman, Louise reasoned. Whoever had typed up the handover sheet might have spelt the name wrong! She was getting worked up over nothing—no doubt the patient in Room 3 would turn out to be a thirty-five-year-old named Danielle with endometriosis.

Silencing the voices in her head, Louise's lips moved into a pale smile—she was just being paranoid.

'Right!' Handover completed, Elaine looked down at her notes then at the team of nurses as she worked out the complicated task of allocating patients. 'Have you had any experience on an acute surgical ward, Louise?'

'Quite a bit.' Louise nodded. 'I worked on a high-dependency—'

'OK,' Elaine cut in, clearly not remotely interested in where Louise had worked before. 'I'll give you some easy ones this morning and then you can help out anywhere else you're needed. Beds 4 through 8 are all due to be discharged after morning rounds, so can you take them, please? Make sure that their discharge letters and drugs are all in order and check that the district nurse has been booked for Mrs Hadlow in bed 5. I'll take beds 1 to 3, though I might need a hand with Jordan in bed 1. He's just out of ICU with a tracheostomy—are you comfortable with tracheostomies? If not,' she said, despite Louise's nod, 'call me or Shona if you're at all concerned.' Louise waited for further patients to be added to her rather paltry workload, but Elaine had already moved on, leaving Louise feeling curiously deflated. For the last couple of weeks she'd dreaded this day, had been reading each and every one of her nursing books and cramming in information, determined not to turn to jelly on her first day back to nursing. And though she knew she should be pleased to be eased in gently, she still felt just a touch disappointed, as if she'd been training for a marathon only to find out it had turned into a rather gentle jog around the park.

'I'll show you around,' Shona offered, and Louise gratefully accepted.

'Don't worry,' Shona said in a dry voice as she took Louise on a quick tour of the ward. 'Elaine's just as *lovely* to everyone on their first day—I think she just likes to make it clear who's the boss.'

'Well, she's made it very clear,' Louise said in an equally dry voice, but with a smile on her face, deciding that she liked Shona.

The other nurse grinned back. 'Right, to business. The whole ward is basically shaped like the letter H—you've got the patients' rooms running along either side. A few single-bedded rooms and some double-rooms with the all the sickest patients are in the middle, near the nurses' station. That's beds 1 to 3 and beds 25 to 28.'

'Is bed 3 very unwell, then?' Louise blushed as she fished for a little more information on the mysterious Danny Ashwood, but Shona just laughed.

'Very embarrassed, I think, would be more apt,' she said cryptically, then carried on with her introduction to the ward. Louise desperately tried to pay attention, but over and over her eyes were drawn to the closed door of Room 3. 'Each corridor is a mirror image of the other and in the middle is the nurses' station, doctors' room and the NUM's office—but Elaine takes it over whenever Candy's off duty. This is the pan room—I'm sure you've seen plenty in your time. The clean room's the one opposite—dressings, IV trolleys, that type of thing. Next door we've got the equipment room, which is kept locked or the other wards nick our IV poles…' They were chatting as they were walking, Shona pointing things out as they went.

'You'll soon get used to it.' They were back to the middle now and both stopped while Louise got her bearings. 'This screen lights up when a patient buzzes—red means it hasn't been answered, green means there's a nurse in attendance. And here's the crash cart. Do you want to go through it? I'm supposed to check it today so it's no trouble to do it now.'

'Please.' Louse nodded. The crash cart would be needed in an emergency, not just when a patient went into cardiac arrest but during any sudden deterioration in their condition, and as an emergency wasn't the ideal time to familiarise herself with the contents, she was glad of the chance to go through it now.

'It's all pretty standard.' Shona pulled out the list and called out the contents as Louise located them and checked for expiry dates and working order. It was a check that was done daily on any ward to ensure the cart was always up to date, and also each time the trolley was checked or used it was signed off by two staff members.

'How long have you worked here?' Louise asked.

'Six months and no time off for good behavior either.' Shona smiled. 'It can be so busy here. Mind you, it's all good experience. Right, if you're happy that you know where everything is, I'd better get on.'

'Sure. Sing out if you need a hand,' Louise offered. 'I'm not exactly going to be rushed off my feet with the patients I've been allocated—they're all about to be discharged!'

'Don't count on it.' Shona rolled her eyes as the patient call-board lit up like a Christmas tree. 'That's two of mine buzzing already.'

'Do you want me to get one?'

'You'd better do your own work first. I'll soon call if I need a hand.'

There was nothing worse than having little to do when everyone else seemed flat out. Elaine was preparing for the doctors' round with the ward clerk as the other nurses were dashing past, looking flustered and busy, but despite Louise's offers to help, everyone seemed to prefer to be busy by themselves than share the load.

Her own patients were all self-caring, the night staff had done all their observations and, checking their files, Louise felt even more at a loose end when she saw that all the meds and discharge orders had been completed.

'Do you want me to give Jordan his wash and meds?' Louise offered as Elaine raced over to grab some X-rays the doctors would need for the ward round, but she shook her head.

'Just leave him. He's had a rough night and only settled off to sleep around four a.m. I'll do him once the ward round's finished.'

Suddenly she smiled and Louise remembered that her first impression of Elaine had been how pretty she was, because when she forgot to frown she looked lovely.

Not that Elaine was smiling at her! Louise didn't even have to look over her shoulder to where Elaine was looking to guess who had just walked through the door.

Holding in a weary sigh Louise made herself scarce as a group of dark suits approached—clearly the Monday morning consultants' round was way above her station.

It hadn't been, though.

Checking her patients' notes for the umpteenth time and trying to look busy, for the first time in the longest time a wave of nostalgia practically knocked her off her feet. Sitting down at the nurses' station, watching the theatre of a busy ward unfolding before her eyes, tears were suddenly appallingly close as she remembered how it had once been.

When she, Louise, had been in charge and taking the consultants' around—when she'd known not just what she was doing, but where she was going in her career. Having spent more than a year in a famous London teaching hospital, she could have walked into any job she had wanted once she had returned to Australia. The surgical nursing world had supposedly been her oyster—but she had met Daniel Ashwood.

If that brief flirting during the ward round hadn't led to a drink, followed by dinner, followed by...

Louise coloured up just at memory, still stunned, all this time later, that she'd tumbled, literally tumbled into bed with him that very night. At the time it had felt so right—the attraction so intense, so completely overwhelming that their first date couldn't have ended any other way. It had been like opening the door to paradise, Louise recalled, but, watching as Elaine giggled girlishly at something one of the consultants had said, a rather nasty smile twisted on her lips. Elaine should be *very* careful what she wished for—even paradise had its drawbacks!

Danny Ashwood.

Staring down at her handover notes—even though she knew it couldn't possibly be him, there was some strange comfort to be had just seeing the name in print—and till she opened the door and confirmed that it was a different person entirely, it was nice to dream for a moment, nice to hold onto that tiny sliver of fantasy that Daniel was close.

For goodness' sake, Louise chided herself for even daring to go there. Daniel Ashwood was the *last* person she wanted to see right now—the very last person she needed complicating her life! Deciding to put herself out of her misery, Louise took action and stood up, heading for the shelf of nursing notes, only to find bed 3's wasn't there. Perhaps they were being used for the ward round, but no. Louise frowned, because only bed 3's slot was empty. All the other nursing files were neatly in place.

Well, she'd just go right ahead and look, Louise decided, just pop her head around the door and ask if everything was OK. Then she could put this stupid fantasy to bed, put Daniel Ashwood firmly out of her mind—where he belonged.

'Did Danny buzz?'

Her hand on the door, jumping as if she'd been caught stealing, Louise froze as Elaine bustled over.

'Sorry.' Louise forced an apologetic smile. 'I got the rooms mixed up. I thought this was Room 4. I was just going to strip the bed now that the patient's gone home.'

'Then it's just as well I stopped you. Danny needs his rest. You're to let me know if he buzzes and *I'll* attend to him. I've just called the orderly to come and prepare Room 4—there's going to be a new admission direct from Theatre, a twenty-two-year-old male with a stab wound to the loin. That's all the information I have. I'll let you know more when I find out.'

'Thanks.' Louise answered easily but her mind was working overtime as she bade farewell to 'Danielle' and tried to fathom Elaine's rather proprietorial response—consoling herself that Elaine had been exactly the same about Jordan. However, for the rest of the morning it was as if the room taunted her. Her obsession with the patient behind the firmly closed door grew, because even if *her* Daniel was safely setting the world on fire in London, this one was clearly something special, too, because it took a trip to the loo, a squirt or perfume and a fresh coat of lipstick for Elaine to even go and take his temperature.

Still, at least Louise had something to do now. Once Room 4 had been cleaned by the orderly, she set about preparing it for the new admission, bringing in the observation trolley and making the bed.

'Getting a new one?' Shona asked, coming in and taking over one side of the bed, both nurses chatting as they tucked in the sheets and blankets in unison.

'Stab wound to the loin,' Louise said. 'He's in Theatre now.' They worked in silence till Louise could take it no more—if she didn't find out, then quite simply she'd burst! 'What's wrong with the patient next door?' Louise asked as casually as she could, hiding her blush as she stuffed a pillow into its case and took great interest in plumping it up. 'I nearly went in by mistake and Elaine said that if the patient even buzzed then she was to be told—is he being barrier-nursed?'

'Oh, no.' Shona laughed. 'Nothing like that. Elaine probably thinks it fitting that only the most senior staff look after him—he's one of our consultants.'

'The patient in Room 3?' Louise croaked.

'Yep.' Shona nodded. 'I think Elaine's trying to dazzle him with a bit of TLC, but she can spray as much perfume and put on as much lipstick as she likes, that's one nut she's not going to crack…' She let out a peel of laughter. 'Pardon the pun.'

'You've lost me.'

'Oh, that's right, you missed handover, didn't you?' Shona checked there was no one around and then leant over the bed and spoke in a low, delighted whisper. 'Well, just in case you do end up going in there, you'd better know that he isn't really abdo pain for investigation—he had a rather painful injury playing cricket yesterday! The Ashwood family jewels are as black as coal, but thankfully saved and in full working order!'

'Sorry?'

'He had a torsion of the testes, the poor guy!' Shona winced and grinned at the same time, crossing her legs as just the thought of it! 'Very nasty. He was operated on yesterday afternoon, then had to return for drainage of a haematoma—he only got back from his second op at six this morning. All the poor guy wants, no doubt, is to go home, not spend the morning flirting. More's the pity, mind you—he's gorgeous!'

'I used to work with a consultant by that name—well, he was called Daniel…' Louise's heart was hammering in her chest as she spoke, torn between hope and dread. 'Mind you, that was in London. There must be loads of doctors…'

'Danny's from London,' Shona shrugged. 'He's on a year's rotation here—maybe it is him!' Oblivious to Louise's expression, she glanced around the room. 'I'll go and get a gown for the new admission and a kidney dish, then you might as well go for your coffee-break before the new admission comes up.'

As surely as if a cricket ball had hit *her* at high speed, Louise felt as if the wind had literally been knocked out of her, could feel her scarlet cheeks paling as the blood literally drained from her face. Shaking, she lowered herself onto the newly made bed and buried her face in her hands, still, at the eleventh hour, trying to reassure herself that it was a simple mistake, that the man in the next room wasn't really Daniel.

And wondering how on earth she'd cope if indeed it was!

'Jordan needs suctioning urgently.' One of the student nurses came racing down the corridor, looking more than a little alarmed. 'His chest sounds terrible.'

Instantly Louise snapped to attention, her personal dilemma completely pushed aside as she heard the note of urgency in the student's voice. 'What happened?' Louise asked, as she made her way swiftly down the ward, because even though it was Elaine's patient, a tracheostomy patient with breathing difficulties couldn't wait for anyone. 'Who's in with him?'

'Just me,' the student started, her voice trailing off as she realised the folly of her ways as she said the words out loud. Louise would need to talk to her about it later. Now wasn't the time or place to tell her never to leave a patient who had difficulty breathing distressed and unattended. Bracing herself for what she might find, hearing his distress from halfway down the corridor, Louise flew the last few steps.

'It's OK, Jordan.' Louise's voice was reassuring as she entered the room, straight away pushing the call bell for further assistance. Pulling on a pair of gloves, she carefully checked his tracheostomy, relieved to see that it was securely in place. From her handover sheet, Louise knew that Jordan had been in a high-impact motor-vehicle accident two months previously—a mixture of booze, dope and high jinks had almost ended his life. Along with abdominal injuries, he had suffered head and facial injuries. The facial injuries had compromised his airway, necessitating a tracheostomy, which he was being weaned off. But the tracheostomy tube could sometimes fall out or, as was the case in this instance, as Louise immediately decided after a brief assessment, a patient's airway could become blocked with a mucous plug. Jordan still had air entry, his chest was moving on inspiration, but the air entry was poor and he was clearly distressed.

Louise turned on the suction machine, checking the soft rubber's patency and lubricating it at the same time with some sterile water, then guided the tube into the airway, placing her finger over the connection to close the circuit and allow the machine to suction the blockage, as Jordan coughed and wheezed.

'His sats are dropping, they're only…' the student said in a alarmed voice as she placed the probe on Jordan's finger. But Louise silenced her with a wide-eyed glare—panic was the very last thing Jordan needed right now.

'It's OK, Jordan,' Louise soothed over the noisy suction machine. 'Give me a big cough and we'll soon have you breathing normally.'

'Good man!' Shona was in the room now, rubbing Jordan's back, assisting him to cough, and Louise was grateful for her calming manner. A compromised airway was a medical emergency and if the partial blockage wasn't shifted quickly then an emergency call would have to be put out, but with tracheostomies, events like this unfortunately weren't unusual. A calm, efficient manner was often more beneficial than having loud overhead chimes and doctors rushing into the room.

'There we go.' The gurgle of the suction machine and the loud whistling cough as she removed the blockage had everyone in the room, especially Jordan, breathing a touch easier.

'How is he?' Elaine's voice was brisk as she swung into the room and pulled on gloves of her own.

'Better now,' Louise said. 'He had a large mucous plug. He's still very gurgly, though—he needs deep suction…'

'I'll do that,' Elaine said, briskly and rather rudely taking over. 'Kelly wants to speak to you.'

'It can wait, Elaine! Louise is obviously busy.' Louise recognised the voice from the doorway as Kelly's, but her words were wasted as a determinedly efficient Elaine took over, clearly feeling *her* skills were what were needed here. Louise peeled off her gloves and washed her hands, before stepping outside.

'Well done,' Kelly said. 'You handled that well—you've clearly worked with trachies before.'

'It doesn't mean I like them.' Louise smiled wryly, only realising now the emergency was over how much it had actually shaken her. 'I've been out of nursing for a few months…'

'That's right. You've got a young baby, haven't you?' The light above her flashed and Louise stood rigid as Kelly paused, clearly expecting Louise to attend to the patient rather than remain talking to her.

'It's Elaine's patient,' Louise said, as Kelly gave her a rather surprised look. 'She said I should let her know if he buzzes. Apparently he's a doctor here.'

'Ah yes.' Kelly nodded and popped her head into Room 4. 'Danny's buzzing, Elaine—I've told Louise to get it.'

Louise could only imagine Elaine's face, but the thought didn't stay. Instead, her heart was racing and she could hear the blood pounding in her ears as she approached the forbidden door, bracing herself for what was on the other side, hoping, knowing she was surely wrong, but somehow wishing she could be right. Every emotion she possessed tumbled in confusion as she pushed open the door and stepped inside because, despite the closed curtains and darkened room, there was no mistaking the face lying on the pillow that turned to face her as she entered—a face she'd seen lying on a pillow so many, many times, but under much kinder circumstances. Her fears, her wishes were all answered crashingly as she stared into familiar, shocked, indigo eyes.

'Hello, Daniel.' She must have said it because she could hear the words fill the shocked silence, but her voice didn't sound like her own, the light-hearted, easy way she'd once greeted him light years from this strained, forced greeting as she stared at the man who had once adored her—the man who had then so cruelly hurt her.

Stared at the father of her son.

CHAPTER TWO

LOUISE!

Daniel didn't say it, just stared at the opening door and the woman walking into his room, his face tightening in disbelief as she paused in the doorway. He tried to convince himself that he must surely be hallucinating as he held back the name that was on the tip of his tongue, had been on the tip of his tongue for ages now. He was terrified of making even more of a fool of himself in front of his colleagues, of calling out her name only to watch his Louise morph into one of the regular nurses on the ward. So instead he blinked a few times, tried to convince himself that it wasn't her—that surely it was the drugs or pain or anaesthetic causing his mind to play tricks.

It couldn't be her!

He didn't want it be Louise, not because he didn't want to see her—hell, she was the reason he was here in Australia after all! He just didn't want her to see him like this. Daniel dragged in a deep breath and forced himself to slam the window shut on memories that were starting to breeze in. Lying in a hospital bed, unwell and disorientated, and completely out of control.

It couldn't be her, Daniel told himself again, because *his* Louise's hair was shorter, her body slimmer, more girlish.

This was a woman—all woman, he noted as she walked slowly towards him, a softer, more curvaceous version of Louise, her familiar, fresh scent dusting his nostrils, mocking him, reminding him again of the relationship he'd so abruptly discarded, those gorgeous, chocolate brown eyes he had known so well staring once again into his. As her voice reached his ears, finally he succumbed—it really was her.

'Louise.' For what had seemed the longest time as she had walked in to the room, he had said nothing, just stared at her as if he was seeing a ghost. Louise was magnanimous enough to acknowledge to herself what a huge shock this must be for him. He was struggling to sit up now, a muscular arm grabbing the bar that hung above the bed, his face grimacing in pain at the sudden movement. Even in the darkened room she could see the lean muscular lines of his body as his untied gown fell off his shoulders.

'God, I thought I was seeing things for a minute. What are you doing here?'

'Working.' She gave a tight smile. 'But given I'm the one who's from Australia, shouldn't I be asking that question of you?'

'I thought you lived out in the country…' He was in obvious pain and if it had been anyone else, without hesitation she'd have moved to help, would have told him to sit forward as she shifted the pillows scattered behind him into a supportive cushion, but she was frozen to the spot in the middle of the room.

'I did,' Louise responded stiffly, but something inside her gave in then, the nurse in her so ingrained that she made her way over, flicked on the overhead light, straightened his pillows, pulled his gown back up over his shoulders then retied the ribbons at the back. Somehow she managed not to touch him or acknowledge the grateful nod as he rested back. 'What did you want?' When he didn't answer, she elaborated. 'You buzzed—is there anything I can help you with?'

'Forget that.' He let out a stunned, incredulous half-laugh. 'I haven't seen you in over a year. Surely—'

'Surely what?' Her eyes challenged him to continue. 'Surely there must be something to talk about? Surely we have some catching up to do?'

'Louise?' His voice was groggy, his pupils constricted from the undoubtedly generous amount of opiates he'd been given post-operatively, and for a sliver of time she actually felt sorry for him. The poor guy had had two rounds of surgery after all, and to wake up to the vengeful face of one's ex wasn't exactly the ideal scenario. But her sympathy lasted about two seconds. Remembering what he'd put her through, the agony of the past few months, Louise was hard pushed to keep a malicious smile off her face as she thought of his injury—in the hell of a lonely pregnancy and birth it was one she'd dreamt of inflicting herself!

'How's your pain?'

'Not too bad,' Daniel said, but from his gritted teeth she knew he was lying. 'I can't believe this—I mean, you being here!'

'On a scale of one to ten,' Louise said, completely ignoring his personal comments and keeping things entirely professional, 'how would you rate your pain?'

'Louise,' Daniel interrupted, 'can we talk about us?'

'Us!' It was Louise now giving a shocked laugh as she shook her head. 'I'll ask again—on a scale of one to ten, how would you rate your pain?'

'Five,' Daniel said. 'And no, I don't want anything else for pain. Louise…'

She didn't let him finish. Her only thought was to get out of the room and somehow attempt to process the fact in her shocked brain that Daniel was here, and it wasn't going to be a fleeting meeting either—he was the consultant of the ward she was working on! She had to get away, had to work out how on earth she was supposed to deal with it.

'I'm busy with another patient now.' She attempted brisk and efficient but it came out rather too harshly and Louise corrected herself—reminding herself that even if it was Daniel, today he was a patient—that today, at least, he deserved her respect and care. 'What did you buzz for?'

'I wanted to find out how long it would be till my discharge meds are ready. I'm really keen to get home.'

Which was understandable, but from the slightly grey tinge to his face and the fact he was still on high-dose analgesics, Louise doubted he'd be going home any time that day. Still, she'd leave it for someone else to break that news to him, she decided. Right now, all she wanted was out.

'I can't answer that for you, Daniel. Elaine's the nurse in charge and she's the one allocated to look after you, but she's busy with another patient right now. As soon as she's done, I'll let her know you were asking.' Managing the briefest of smiles, she turned to go, but the drugs he was on must have weakened his usual staunch reserve because she hadn't even reached the door before he called out to her.

'That's it? You're just going to walk out like that? You've nothing else to say?'

She had *nothing* else to say—nothing that could be said, without breaking down anyway—twelve months of hell ripping through her as with the briefest shake of her head

Louise walked out of his room, scarcely able to comprehend the appalling coincidence that had bought Daniel Ashwood back into her life.

'What did Danny want?' Elaine practically pounced on her as she walked out of the room—not that Louise noticed, her mind spinning at the shocking confrontation, stunned, appalled, terrified not just that he was here but that, despite all that had happened, despite all the dirty water under their bridge, somehow she still wanted him.

'Louise,' Elaine insisted. 'What did Danny want?'

'He wants to know when his discharge meds will be ready.' Running a dry tongue over her pale lips, Louise forced herself to act normally. 'I think he wants to go home.'

'Well, he's not going anywhere. The surgeons want him to stay for another twenty-four hours—I'd better go and break the news. Are you OK?'

'I'm fine,' Louise said, then, seeing Elaine's frown, thought she'd better come up with a reason. 'I'm a bit sore, actually— I've never gone this long without feeding Declan.'

'I know you didn't get a coffee-break—why don't you have an early lunch?' Elaine offered. 'Add your coffee-break to it. Theatre just rang and they're going to be keeping that stab wound in Recovery for another hour or so—his blood pressure's still very low.'

Louise didn't need to be asked twice, so she headed down to the crèche and stepped into the hubbub of children's cries and chatter. The room was a den of activity as toddlers messily ate their lunch at low tables and babies banged spoons for attention in their high chairs. But Louise had eyes only for one child in the room, an anxious smile breaking out on her face as Jess, the cheery child-care worker who had greeted her early that morning, ushered her into a chair. 'Someone's going to be very pleased to see you.' Jess beamed. 'He's just woken up from his morning nap. Have a seat and I'll get him for you.'

The sight of Declan's angry red face as Jess brought him over tore at her heartstrings, her breasts literally aching for her son. 'Did he take the bottle OK this morning?' Louise asked anxiously.

'It took a while.' Jess gave a sympathetic smile at Louise's distraught face. 'He'll soon get used to it and remember that it's your milk that we're giving him.' Her tone was reassuring. 'Don't feel guilty for having to work. Like I said, he'll soon get used to it.'

He had no choice *but* to get used to it, Louise thought, wishing it didn't have to be like this. She took her red-faced, tearful son from Jess, her breasts weeping as he was handed over, hating the thought of him crying for her while she worked just a short distance away. Rage starting to trickle in that her tiny baby had to be in a crèche rather than at home, where he belonged at this tender age.

Yes, rage, Louise decided as slowly her baby calmed, as slowly he relaxed in her arms and hungrily took his feed. Rage that Daniel Ashwood had done this to her.

Had done this to them.

'Danny wants to talk to you.' Elaine's face looked as if she'd been sucking lemons as she reluctantly passed on the message. 'I told him you were in the crèche, feeding your son, but he said that he'd like a word when you came back.'

'You told him…' Louise snapped her mouth closed. Panic built inside her, which she tried hard not to let Elaine see. 'What did he say?'

'I've already told you,' Elaine answered tartly, turning on her rubber-soled heel. 'And can you make it quick please? When you're done, I want you to give an enema to bed 2.'

If Elaine considered it a punishment, she was wrong—giving an enema was infinitely preferable to answering Daniel's inevitable questions. Deep down she'd known this day was coming, just never in her wildest dreams when she'd woken up that morning had she thought it might be this one. Over the last twelve months she had penned so many unsent letters to him, and she wished she had one of them in her pocket now, could hand it to him to read, could let him know, without breaking down, why it had been so impossible to tell him she was pregnant, why she'd made the difficult decision to raise Declan alone.

Bracing herself, she opened the door, her usually sunny face pale and grim, her mind whirring as to how to play this, how to deal with the barrage of fire that was surely heading her way.

'You wanted to talk to me?'

'I think there's quite a bit to say.' The calmness in his voice caught her completely unawares. He looked much more together now. His bed had been freshly made, the curtains were open and his eyes more able to focus. 'Don't you?'

'Not really.' Louise gave a tight shrug, unsure where this was leading, confused by his demeanour. 'I think you made things very clear the last time we spoke,'

'Sit down, Louise,' Daniel said, and then softened it slightly. 'Please.' It was easier to sit than stand, so she did so, utterly unable to look at him, terrified that if she did she'd start crying. 'I just think it would be better if we clear the air now.'

Clear the air?

Her eyes darted to his, then darted away, her mind struggling to fathom his meaning.

'We're obviously going to be working together and things might get a bit uncomfortable if—'

'Don't worry,' Louise broke in. 'I'm not going to walk around with a megaphone, telling everyone I shagged the new consultant last year when I was on a working holiday.'

'Louise,' Daniel snapped like a schoolmaster. 'There's no need for language like that.'

'Why not?' Louise shrugged. 'That's exactly what it was, according to you—a quick fling with no involvement!'

'I said some harsh things when we broke up,' Daniel said a touch less loftily. 'A lot of them I wish I could take back. I never meant to imply—'

'You didn't imply anything, Daniel,' Louise interrupted. 'You spelt things out—very clearly, in fact. And for the record, *we* didn't break up. If I remember rightly, you woke up one morning—after we'd spent a night making love, I hasten to add—and told me that it was never going to work, that I wasn't the sort of wife you wanted—'

'Louise, listen—'

'No, Daniel, you listen!' She'd grown up in a year, the dizzy, happy-go-lucky girl he'd met gone for ever as the woman she now was turned her eyes to face him. 'You told me that the last thing you wanted from me was a serious relationship, that you'd thought we were just having a "bit of fun" before I went back to Australia…'

'Louise.' His calm voice only exacerbated her agitated one. 'Clearly we did both want different things. I just felt that it was all moving too quickly. Yes, that night we had made love, but that night you had also made it clear that somewhere in the not-too-distant future you wanted a husband and babies.'

'I didn't say that!' Louise said indignantly. 'God, you make it sound as if I was desperate. If you care to remember, we were talking about where we saw ourselves in five years. I'd have been thirty-two by then…'

'And I'd have been thirty-nine.' Daniel shrugged. 'And I realised that night we had different visions of our futures. It was just all getting too serious. Louise, you were talking of extending your stay in the UK because of me, because of us!'

'Because I thought there was an us,' Louise choked. 'Because I thought you felt as strongly as I did. I thought we wanted the same thing.'

'Well, we didn't,' Daniel broke in, shattering her already broken heart just a touch further, if that were possible. 'Clearly! Elaine mentioned you had a baby now…' Louise sucked in her breath, every nerve taut, staring at his expressionless face and trying to fathom what he was thinking, trying to work out her answer to the question that was surely, after all this time, coming. 'And I'm glad for you,' Daniel said, oblivious to the bewildered frown spreading over her face. 'I'm pleased that you've found someone who makes you happy. I just wanted to be sure there were no hard feelings between us, given that we're going to be working together.'

She couldn't believe what she was hearing, had truly thought she was walking in the room to defend herself, to listen as he berated her for not telling him about their child, but instead he was wishing her and her supposed partner well!

'That's what you called me in to say?' Her voice was shrill, her eyes blinking rapidly as she tried to take in what he was saying. She couldn't believe that his denial could be so firmly

ingrained. God, they'd been together a year ago and she had
a three-month-old baby—how could it not even entered his
head that Declan might well be his? Did he think she'd walked
straight out of his bed and into someone else's who could give
her what she had apparently so badly wanted? 'Daniel, I have
a three-month-old baby—'

'What did you call him?' Daniel interrupted with that curiously snobby voice he used when he was addressing a
patient or member of staff and keeping them at a distance.

'Declan.' She shook her head as if to clear it, stared at him
open-mouthed, waiting—for what she didn't know, revelation,
realization? She truly didn't know. But he just stared back.

'And you're happy?' Daniel asked, and she felt his eyes
drift down to her hand, clearly taking in the naked ring finger.
'I mean, you and his father—'

'It didn't work out between us.' Finding her voice, she
responded with the truth. 'You know me—I've got lousy
taste in men.'

He gave a pale smile at her thinly disguised insult. 'So
you're on your own?'

She gave a nod, stared into the eyes of the man she had
loved absolutely and wished to God she could hate him.

'It certainly looks that way!'

'You *have* to tell him!'

Pouring two glasses of wine, Maggie pushed one towards
Louise. 'And don't tell me you can't have a drink because
you're feeding—this is strictly medicinal!'

'Believe me, I'm not going to.' Taking a sip, Louise let out
a long, exaggerated sigh, utterly exhausted physically from
her first long day back at work and drained emotionally from

the never-ending roller-coaster ride she'd embarked on the day she'd laid eyes on Daniel Ashwood.

'They call him Danny!'

'Of course they do.' Maggie grinned. 'I was Margaret until I met you—you Aussies change everyone's names!'

'You really didn't know he was working there?' Louise checked, her eyes narrowing in suspicion, but Maggie shook her head.

'I'm as stunned as you are! Come on, Louise, it's a massive hospital and there's not exactly a huge demand for surgeons in the psychiatric ward—it's not just the patients that are shut off from the rest of the world in the psych unit.'

'I can't believe he's working in the same hospital. I mean, of all the places he could have ended up…'

'That's the only bit that's not so hard to believe,' Maggie said. 'Come on, Louise, when you decided to move to the city, why did you pick Melbourne General?'

'Because it's the biggest hospital, because it has everything…'

'Someone of Daniel's calibre was hardly going to end up in a 200-bed suburban hospital,' Maggie pointed out. 'It's why he's in Australia that intrigues me! He has to know, Louise.'

'He doesn't want to know!' Louise snapped, and then regretted it. 'I'm sorry, Maggie, I don't mean to take it out on you. I just can't believe it didn't even enter his head that Declan could be his! I'm serious,' she said as Maggie gave her a very disbelieving look. 'He wasn't avoiding the issue— he honestly didn't seem to think there could possibly be one!'

'He's a doctor, for heaven's sake,' Maggie argued. 'You don't have to be a mathematical genius to work out that you broke up last year and you've got a three-month-old baby!'

'Ah, but I was out for a good time!' Louise said with a distinct edge to her voice. 'According to Daniel's thinking, Declan could be anyone's!' Tears filled Louise's eyes. 'Is that what he thinks of me?'

'It's what he thinks of himself that worries me,' Maggie said cryptically. 'Louise, you have to look after yourself here. Stop trying to work out what he's thinking—I don't think you're ever going to really know.'

'When we were together,' Louise gulped, closing her eyes at the bitter-sweet memory, 'I felt as if I'd found my soul-mate. I can remember seeing him on the ward that first time I did the doctors' round—all aloof and snooty in his suit, just as he always was with everyone—then we did the ward round, and it was the first time I'd actually spoken to him, probably the first time he ever really looked at me. I remember saying something and he laughed, and I knew from everyone's reaction that he was acting out of character. I just knew from the little I'd seen of him that he was distant and not very friendly, but with me he was like another person.'

'He adored you,' Maggie said gently, as a massive salty tear rolled down Louise's cheek.

'After that ward round he came back and I knew he was going to ask me out. I was just so completely and utterly sure that he'd come back…'

'And he did.' Maggie nodded.

'It wasn't just about having a good time and some sort of casual holiday fling,' Louise insisted, despite the fact Maggie wasn't disputing what she said, despite the evidence to the contrary, despite Daniel telling her face to face that it had been just that. 'Those four weeks we were together were the closest I've ever been to another person, and Daniel can deny it all he likes but I know that at the time he felt it, too. I just don't know why he suddenly changed his mind.'

'Look, all you can do here is watch out for yourself. Frankly, I'm all for telling him. If he doesn't want to offer emotional support then slug him for the financial. After all, he can afford it and you *do* need the money.'

'I don't,' Louise insisted. 'I've got three months' work pencilled in, I'm doing fine.'

'Are you?' Maggie checked. 'You've got a pile of bills stuffed behind the microwave—'

'As soon as I get paid, they'll be gone,' Louise swiftly retorted, but Maggie just stared. 'And I'm going to start looking for a place this weekend.' She felt a twinge at the thought of not living with Maggie any more, but while their small flat was fine for two single girls living a carefree existence, it wasn't suitable for raising a child and had only ever been a stopgap for her. 'In a few weeks things will be fine. Fine,' she said again, as if by repeating it she was somehow assuring it would all happen.

'Declan's dad is a consultant surgeon,' Maggie said softly. 'He's raking it in.'

'I know,' Louise gulped, 'and sometimes it terrifies me. Sometimes I think I should take him for everything he's worth because Declan deserves it.'

'And other times?' Maggie pushed gently.

'I look at my parents—their marriage ended because of a brief affair my father had six months before he met my mum. Every month a fight broke out when it was time for Dad to pay his maintenance—'

'Louise—' Maggie attempted, but Louise stopped her right there.

'Daniel and I were together for four weeks,' Louise said. 'I don't want him paying for his mistake for the rest of his life, the way my dad did.'

'Even if you have to?'

'That's the difference.' Ignoring her wine, Louise stood up, wandered over to the tiny kitchenette and flicked on the kettle. 'I don't see it as a mistake. Yes, Daniel may be a consultant, but clearly he didn't think I'd make a very good consultant's wife. This is about so much more than money.'

'What if he asks you out now?'

'As if!' Louise scoffed. 'And even if he did, there's no way I'd go.'

'Why not?'

Louise thought for a moment before answering. 'Because I can't imagine trying to fill him in on the last year of my life and somehow managing to omit the fact that Declan's his.'

'Would it be the end of the world if he found out?'

'The end of his world probably. He doesn't want children.'

'But he's got one! And if things don't work out between the two of you, at the very least you know he's a decent guy and you'll have some financial support. Louise, lies catch up in the end and you're living with a time bomb. A cute one at that.'

'Well, it isn't going to happen. According to Daniel, I'm a single mother, which is hardly an upcoming young consultant's ideal date.'

'Don't be so sure!' Never one to miss an opportunity, Maggie picked up Louise's still full glass. 'There's a lot of unfinished business there—for both of you.'

CHAPTER THREE

'SORRY if this is awkward for you!'

A good dose of Maggie had an infinitely calmer Louise steering her stainless-steel dressing trolley into Daniel's room the next morning. With Elaine on a late shift, staff allocation had been done by the nurse unit manager, Candy, who, blissfully unaware of their history, had decided, given the nature of Daniel's injury, to save him the embarrassment of having someone familiar look after him and had allocated the delicate task of taking his dressing down to a blushing Louise.

'Awkward doesn't come close.' Daniel grimaced, wobbling his way gingerly back to the bed with his IV pole in one hand, a pair of black cycling-short-style undies on and a white T-shirt at mid-torso and pulled onto one arm only. 'That's why I took the dressing down myself in there.'

'Have you had a shower?' Louise said accusingly, answering the question for herself as she did so—his hair was drenched and his back was still soaking. 'You're not supposed to get your dressing wet—and you know that you're supposed to let the staff know if you get out of bed. You could have passed out or anything.'

'I'd have been far more likely to pass out if you'd come at

me with those bloody tweezers and peeled it off…' Daniel attempted, but his face had a horribly greyish tinge and Louise knew that, despite his bravado, the room was spinning for him. She watched as beads of sweat broke out on his forehead and knew that if he didn't get to the bed soon, he'd end up on the floor. 'Come on,' she said gently, taking the IV pole from him and instinctively taking his arm—instinctively, because she was a nurse and he was a patient who had done way too much and was about to pass out. But nothing in her nursing career had prepared her for this, his touch, the first in almost a year almost more than she could bear, feeling his reluctant weight on her arm as she tried to lead him the short distance to his bed.

Maybe her touch was too much for him, too, because after a few seconds of contact he pulled away. But Louise was having none of it.

'Take my arm and let's get you back to bed,' Louise said firmly, but again he pushed it away, attempting to drag himself the last few steps. However, his body today wasn't as autonomous as his mind, and he clutched at a chair to steady himself, loudly dragging in air as he willed himself not to faint. Completely unfazed, Louise just rolled her eyes.

'Faint away, then, Daniel.'

'I'm OK,' he insisted through very pale, very dry lips.

'The porters can always help me lift you back into bed when you land on the floor…'

He gave in then, actually held out his hand to her, and she took not just that, but his arm, too, placing her other arm around his. His back was drenched with cold sweat as she swiftly steered his fall from grace onto the safety of the mattress—and he lay there on his side for a moment, ghastly pale and completely out of it. If she'd been more junior she'd have pressed the bell and called for help, but Louise was confident enough in her own ability to know that Daniel was suffering from nothing more than a simple faint, and saved him the indignity of the world rushing in by raising the foot of the bed and giving him a quick whiff of oxygen. She checked his pulse and watched him closely as he came round.

Yes, she'd giggled with Maggie about the appropriateness of his injury, made more than a few wicked comments last night as she'd compared it to childbirth, but watching this tall proud man absolutely out of it, seeing the purple bruise halfway down his inner thigh and spreading over the top of his cycle shorts, she softened like butter, knowing how horrible and undignified this entire episode must have been for him. Despite the pain, despite the anger, she actually felt sorry for him.

'You fainted,' Louise said gently, as his eyes slowly opened. 'But you're fine now.'

'Did you call a code?' Even in this wretched state he managed a stab of dry humour at his predicament. 'Just in case there's someone left in the hospital who's missed out on a good look at my scrotum!'

'Ooh, believe me, I thought about it,' Louise grinned down at him and watched as a ghost of a smile flickered on his lips, standing quietly as his colour slowly returned and his pulse settled. 'Better?' she said finally, when she'd checked his blood pressure. Clearly he was, so she turned off the oxygen and lowered the foot of the bed as he slowly sat up.

'Thanks.' Daniel nodded, letting out a long breath. 'Thanks,' he said again, clearly appreciating the fact that it was still just the two of them in the room.

'Have some water,' she offered, splashing some water from

the jug into a beaker and lifting it to his lips, knowing as surely as the sun rose every morning that if it had been anyone else other than her who had walked into the room, they'd have been shooed away with a stern bark, and he'd have ended up on the floor. She was glad for the chance to be able to look after him—at least for this short time.

'How's your pain?' Louise asked. 'And, please, don't fob me off.'

'Between you and me?' he said.

'Sure.'

'Bloody agony,' he admitted. 'But if I have another jab of pethidine, I know that they'll want to keep me in till after lunch.'

'What about a couple of Panadeine Forte,' Louise offered, checking through his chart. 'You're written up—'

'A couple of tablets aren't going to help,' Daniel retorted, proving that doctors really did make the worst patients!

'Well, they definitely won't if you don't take them,' Louise pointed out. 'Why does it have to be all or nothing with you—that if you can't have pethidine then you'll just have to suffer on?'

'OK,' he bristled as Louise marched out and returned a couple of moments later with two white tablets, which he reluctantly swallowed.

'You're too damn proud for your own good!' she scolded, hoping for bossy nurse mode, trying to keep a grip here as she attempted the impossible—to treat him solely as a patient. 'And what on earth have you done with your T-shirt?'

'I couldn't work out how to feed the drip through—you nurses make it look easy.'

Louise collected a towel from the bathroom and then dried his back, before turning off the IVAC and dismantling the IV, pulling the tubing through the free arm of his T-shirt then feeding his hand through.

'This is probably coming down after the round.'

'Hope so,' Daniel said. 'I just want to go home. Is it awkward for you?' He looked up at her. 'Looking after me, I mean?'

She even managed to laugh. 'Not at all! I'm a bit miffed, actually—I was kind of looking forward to giving you a good dressing down!'

'Sweet revenge?' Daniel asked, a hint of a smile ghosting on his pale lips.

'Something like that,' Louise answered. 'I ought to check your wound really, but if you'd rather leave it for the round, I understand.'

'I'll leave it, thanks.'

'Sure,' Louise said, quietly relieved. The thought of seeing him so black and bruised held no appeal. 'I'll just do your obs again.

'Aren't cricketers supposed to wear a shield or something?' she asked as she wrapped the blood-pressure cuff around his arm.

'It's called a box,' Daniel answered. 'And, yes, the *batsman* wears a box, only I wasn't batting at the time—I was supposed to be fielding.'

'I didn't know you played cricket.'

'I don't play much, but an Englishman in Australia has to defend his honour.' He smiled, then changed the subject back from vaguely friendly to painfully personal. 'So, how come you're here, Louise?'

'There wasn't really much work back home—well, not with the hours that I wanted,' Louise said, giving him her standard response, but Daniel knew her too well to be fobbed off.

'It must be hard in the city with your family so far away,' he delved, and as Louise rolled her eyes he gave a low laugh. 'They're not *still* fighting?'

'You've no idea.' Louise gave a dramatic sigh. 'Catherine's getting married in a few months.'

'Your sister?'

'My *half*-sister,' Louise corrected him.

'How's your mum taking it?' he asked, matching her grimace, and it was so nice that even after all this time he understood, so very nice to put the animosity on hold and talk to him again.

To talk as they once had.

'Terribly,' Louise admitted. 'Though, in her defence, there's just no escaping it—in a small country town a wedding's a big thing, especially this one. The local baker's doing the cake, Mum's close friend is a dressmaker and she's working on the wedding dress and all the bridesmaids' outfits, and the reception is being held in the local pub. You'd think it was European royalty that was getting married…'

'That's your mother talking!' Daniel checked, and Louise laughed as she nodded.

'Well, she found out a couple of months ago that Dad was paying for the wedding and even though they're divorced, even though financially it doesn't affect Mum a bit—well, let's just say it wasn't exactly a soothing environment with a new baby on board. I think I'll be staying in Melbourne for a while, at least until after the wedding!'

'So how are things—how are you finding the ward?'

'Good.' Louise nodded. 'I'm starting to find my way around.'

'Who are you looking after this morning?'

'A couple of easy ones—or they would be easy if they didn't go taking showers and fainting on me and then…' She gave an uncomfortable shrug. 'I shouldn't really be discussing the patients.'

'They're *my* patients,' Daniel pointed out. 'Who else have you got?'

'Jordan Adams,' Louise answered.

'How's he doing now he's on the ward?'

'OK,' Louise answered thoughtfully. 'Well, he seems OK. He's being weaned off the tracheostomy and he's starting to eat a little…'

'How's his mood?' Daniel asked perceptively, because it was Jordan's mood that was worrying Louise most. Most patients, after coming out of ICU, were so used to the intense one-on-one nursing contact that they tended to panic once on the ward and demand attention, but instead Jordan's mood was flat, making little eye contact when Louise tried to talk to him, refusing to see his friends when they arrived to visit him—instead, just staring unseeingly at the television above his bed.

'It's not great,' Louise sighed. 'I think he saw himself in the mirror for the first time over the weekend and he hates that colostomy with a passion.'

'Poor kid.' Daniel's voice was pensive. 'Tell him he won't look like that for ever and that we should be able to reverse the colostomy in the not-too-distant future.'

'Of course.' Louise frowned—she didn't need to be told how to look after her patient! 'I've already told him that—several times, in fact.'

'Don't go getting all offended on me,' Daniel said. 'I just want someone to keep reiterating to him that this will pass. A lot of the staff will be busy avoiding the issue, trying to buoy him up and telling him that he's looking fine when the truth is that Jordan looks a fright at the moment—and he knows it!'

'Fair enough.' Louise nodded. 'I'd better get back out there, but first I need to fill in your discharge form.'

'Are you in charge today?'

'Hardly!'

'How come?' Daniel frowned. 'I thought Candy was on this morning. She generally hits her office once the ward round is done and leaves the most senior in charge.'

'Shona's in charge,' Louise explained, but Daniel's frown deepened.

'But you're way more qualified,' he started, but Louise shook her head.

'I'm a bank nurse—I'm really just another pair of hands.'

'An extremely qualified pair of hands,' Daniel argued. 'I'll talk to Candy.'

'Please, don't.' Louise smiled at his rather indignant tone. 'It suits me fine—I've got enough on my mind without stressing about work, and anyway I need to be able to leave the ward to feed Declan.'

'How is he?'

'Loud,' Louise said. 'Maggie says he's testing me and that I should leave him to cry a bit longer.'

'Maggie Johnson?'

'She's here in Melbourne, too, posing as a nurse and sharing a flat with me. Right, that's enough chatting—let's get on with this form.'

'I liked Maggie,' Daniel said, ignoring her attempt to shift the conversation. 'It would be nice to see her, to catch up on the old days. After all, they were good times, weren't they, Lou?' he continued softly, reverting to the name he'd once called her, catching her eyes and holding her gaze for maybe a second or two.

But even if it was fleeting it told her more than she needed to know, dragged her back into vortex of confusion he so readily generated, told her troubled mind that he still had feelings for her, that Maggie's intuition had again proved right and there was unfinished business between them—and not just Declan either.

She needed to get out, needed to put some space between them, to assimilate her thoughts into some sort of sensible order. Ignoring his rather more intimate tone, Louise picked up her pen and scribbled down his obs, shooting him her best professional smile as she started to tick off the annoying but necessary discharge list that had to be completed, even if the patient was a surgical consultant!

'Right, I've got your meds from the pharmacy—and you've got an appointment to come back on Friday for suture removal.'

'Thank you.'

Trying not blush, trying not to care about his answer, she moved to the next part of the form. 'Is there anyone at home to look after you?'

'No,' Daniel answered. 'And neither do I have a handrail over my bath or steps up to my front door. Is this really necessary? I'm a thirty-five-year-old who's had minor surgery, not a seventy-year-old whose had a hip replacement!'

'Rules are rules.' Louise couldn't help but grin. 'Just answer the questions, please.'

'Fine,' Daniel sighed, nodding and shaking his head as she zipped through the list.

'Right, if you don't go fainting again, you should be ready to go when you get the say so. Buzz if you need anything.'

'I won't, hopefully I'll be out of here in the next hour or so.'

'And next time wear your box.'

'Next time I'll make sure the match is being held on the other side of town so when I'm bundled into a car and whisked off to hospital, I end up where no one knows me. It hasn't exactly been the most dignified couple of days!'

'You've enjoyed every moment.' Louise winked without thinking and again slipped back easily into ways of old. 'I bet you're secretly delighted that you've given everyone from porter to consultant an inferiority complex!'

He stared at her with a shocked smile, the same one he'd given her so many times in the past. For such a sophisticated, worldly man he was so very shockable. When they'd been together he'd laughed at her jokes as if they had been the funniest, the rudest and the most original in the world—as if she'd somehow invented humour, as if she, Louise, had held the key to his universe.

'Sorry.' She gave an embarrassed smile, stunned at her own familiarity. Signing off the form, she replaced his charts then collected the trolley and started to wheel it out.

'Louise.'

She was halfway to the door, feeling horribly unsure.

'I'm sorry. Sorry for—'

'Please, don't, Daniel,' Louise broke in, knowing if she was going to get out of that room without breaking down, if she was going to work alongside him and survive, she had to keep things together now. Yesterday's little outburst could never be repeated. She had to keep things as light as they could be, and with a supreme effort she looked him in the eye and managed a tiny dismissive shrug. 'We had a good time, while it lasted. And just in case it's worrying you, I haven't said anything to the ward…well, I mentioned to Shona that I recognised your name but—'

'You don't have to pretend we didn't happen, Louise. I'm not ashamed of it.'

She didn't say anything. Instead she wheeled her trolley out and, closing the door softly behind her, headed to the treatment room. Alone, she let out the breath she'd been holding since she'd closed the door, tears spilling down her cheeks as finally, angrily she answered him.

'Aren't you, Daniel?'

CHAPTER FOUR

'GOOD morning, Jordan.'

At the sound of Daniel's voice, Louise gave the young patient she'd been washing a reassuring smile as the throng of doctors approached the bed. 'I'm Daniel Ashwood, I'm your consultant. I saw you a lot on Intensive Care, but you probably won't remember much of your time there—I operated on you a couple of times when you first came in.' His introduction was formal but informative and though Jordan didn't even attempt a response or look particularly fazed, Louise could sense his embarrassment as the young man was lost somewhere in the middle of myriad hospital personnel and a complicated conversation that took place way over his shaved head.

On his first day back at work since his accident and despite an injury that would have had most men blushing and lying low, Daniel Ashwood had marched into the ward with the same commanding presence that had enthralled Louise when she'd first met him in London.

Immaculate in a navy suit, his dark hair had been cut since the previous week, accentuating the high slant of his cheekbones. Freshly shaven, his masculine fragrance was overwhelmingly familiar as he stood with his registrar, looking over some CT scans and X-rays before the Monday morning round started. Louise had been aware he was on the ward even before she'd seen him! And though she'd spent the last hour or so ducking for cover as best she could and trying to avoid him, inevitably their paths had finally crossed, and though it would have been far more comfortable for Louise to nip out until the ward round had moved on, Jordan's strained face had made her stay. His patchy attempts at conversation were more easily translated by Louise, who after a week of caring for him understood the breathless voice he was developing now his tracheostomy had been removed.

'He's lost another kilo in weight.' Daniel frowned down at the chart he was reading. 'When was the last time the dietician saw him?'

'On Friday,' Candy answered. 'But she was reluctant to increase his nasogastric feeds because it just makes him less hungry at mealtimes—we've been giving him bolus feeds after his meals.'

Ensuring adequate nutrition for a patient as severely injured as Jordan was a constant juggling act. His emaciated body required a high-protein, high-calorie intake, but his poor swallowing ability, combined with his lethargy, made getting the necessary nutrients into him an ongoing battle. His rather paltry intake was being supplemented via his nasogastric tube with fortified fluids, but the rich formula was causing problems with his colostomy as well as reducing his already sluggish appetite and the staff were trying, with little success, to encourage Jordan to make up his calorie deficit himself.

'How's your swallowing now, Jordan?' Daniel asked, his frown remaining as Jordan gave a tired shrug. 'OK. I'm just going to have a look at you.' Gently he prodded Jordan's stomach, his hands working down the young man's skinny legs, testing his reflexes before sitting him forward and listening for a long time to the back of his chest. Louise saw his eyes narrow as he look at the painful cystic acne on Jordan's back, but his smile was kind as he laid him back on his mountain of pillows.

'You've been through the mill a bit, haven't you?' Jordan's lack of response to his question didn't faze Daniel, and he turned to the physio.

'How's his walking?'

'It's coming along,' she responded brightly. 'He's transferring from the bed to the chair and he's managing to walk to the door with a lot of encouragement.'

'Let's get a walking machine up to the room.'

'He's not quite ready for that.' A very white smile from the physio practically dazzled Louise, but Daniel didn't even blink.

'On the contrary, if he can walk to the door he can manage a minute on the walker, and I think it would be very encouraging for Jordan to have one in the room. So can you arrange it, please? And some light weights, too. He can start doing some upper-body work. And I'd like more aggressive physio for Jordan, please—perhaps two sessions a day.'

'OK!'

'Good.' Daniel turned his attention to the dietician. 'And no bolus feeds after meals—Jordan's to achieve his calorie intake himself and any deficit can be made up at night, after visiting hours.' He turned to Jordan. 'Get your friends to bring you in some milkshakes from the take-away.'

'Jordan's not too keen on visitors at the moment,' Louise volunteered, wishing she didn't have to draw Daniel's attention to her, but knowing for her patient's sake she had to. Jordan was sinking rapidly into depression and if his consultant wasn't armed with all the facts, it only made the prognosis more difficult. But as Daniel gave her a brief nod, Louise just knew, from working with him previously and their brief conversation the week before, that Daniel had already guessed as much.

'Does he have the same nursing staff looking after him as far as is possible?'

'Pretty much,' Candy said. 'We're trying to give him some continuity of care—and Louise is rostered for early shifts this month so I've allocated him to her.'

'Right, Jordan, I'm going to have a word with my colleagues outside—I'm sure the last thing you need is us talking over you—but I'll come back and speak with you later and I can go through all your surgery and progress with you.' As the entourage drifted off, Louise picked up Jordan's washcloth, ready once the door had closed to resume washing him, but Daniel had other ideas. 'Louise, could you join us, please?'

Candy was clearly surprised at Louise being invited to such an important party but, then, she'd have no idea that Daniel had worked with her before when she'd had a much more senior role. Blushing a bit, Louise followed the group outside and Daniel closed the door before addressing her.

'How's his mood been this week?'

'Flat,' Louise answered. 'And getting worse. He's just broken up with his girlfriend, Sally.'

'Am I right in assuming it wasn't Jordan's choice?' Daniel asked, hitting the nail on the head, and Louise nodded.

'She told him it was over a couple of days ago. She was there every step of the way apparently for the first few weeks in

Intensive Care, but when he came to and she realised just how serious his injuries were, she just couldn't seem to deal with it.'

'Great timing.' Daniel whistled through his teeth and Louise's eyes widened a touch at his rather angry response as she relayed the facts.

'I've tried to be encouraging and I'm trying to get him to do things for himself, but with limited success.'

'Has he had a psychiatric consultation?' Daniel asked Luke Evans, his registrar, who coloured a little as he shook his head.

'Not yet—he still isn't able to talk very well.'

'I'm sure the psychiatrist is more than capable of reading his notes!' Daniel snapped. 'Two months ago he was out surfing; now he's woken up to find he's got left-sided weakness thanks to a bleed on the brain, a colostomy bag, and his girlfriend's just dumped him because of it! What the hell are you waiting for—a written invitation?'

'I just thought—'

'No,' Daniel broke in, and froze him with a glare. 'Clearly, you didn't think! What about a dermatology review?'

'Sorry?' Luke answered, clearly wishing the ground would just open up and swallow him.

'He's got the worst acne I've seen in ages. Surely you've noticed.'

'O-of c-course,' Luke stammered. 'But surely his acne's the least of his problems.'

'He's nineteen,' Daniel said sharply. 'And while we might not know how Jordan's feeling right now, we can all remember being nineteen, I hope, and I'm sure you'd agree that solving painful, unsightly cystic acne would be near the top of a young man's wish list—can we at least do that for him?'

'Of course,' Luke flustered as Daniel strode off to the next room, his voice trailing off as he rushed behind his boss. 'I just never thought to…'

Most doctors wouldn't, Louise thought to herself, feeling just a little bit sorry for Luke as she headed back into Jordan's room. But, then, Daniel had never been like most doctors. In some ways his bedside manner could be brusque. He'd had Louise wincing on more than a few occasions, touchy-feely certainly not words that would describe him, yet he was the most objective doctor she had ever worked with. He didn't just see the patient or their injury, but looked at the entire picture and utilised every available tool to look after anyone in his care. Whether he realised it or not, Jordan was very lucky to have Daniel Ashwood as his doctor.

'Do you want to go to first lunch?' Candy asked, as Louise attempted to write up her notes. Monday mornings were always busy on any ward, but Daniel's thorough ward round had generated a lot of extra work for everyone. Any thing that might have been missed in his absence had been spotted and was duly being fixed. The phlebotomist was walking around with her trolley and shaking her head in bewilderment at the mountain of blood tests that awaited her, the physiotherapists were all racing around, more junior doctors were writing up the drug orders and treatment regimes that had been changed. In fact, the whole ward was a flurry of noisy activity as everyone caught up with Daniel's exacting standards, so much so that Louise hadn't even managed to get to the crèche to feed Declan. Her so-called break was taken at the nurses' station, juggling the telephone and a pile of nursing notes.

'Please,' Louise answered gratefully, desperate to get to the crèche and feed Declan. Her breasts felt as if they were made of cement, and painful cement at that! 'I'll just finish writing up this last patient.'

'Could I borrow you for a moment, please, Louise?'

Daniel's voice made her jump. Since the ward round he'd disappeared and she hadn't expected to see him again, but here he was, tapping his fingers impatiently on the bench, dressed in theatre gear and looking suitably divine.

'I've got an afternoon theatre list and it's no doubt going to go well into the evening, so I'd like a word with Jordan now or I might not get a chance later.'

'Sure,' Louise said. Daniel turned to go, but she gave a tiny eye roll to Candy as she stood up.

'Go as soon as you're done,' Candy said sympathetically. 'You can finish the notes when you get back!'

'Were you about to do something?'

'Just lunch,' Louise answered easily.

'Sorry to mess up your plans,' Daniel said, with more than a hint of sarcasm.

'I wasn't complaining.'

'Louise, I saw you roll your eyes at Candy. The fact is, if I don't speak to Jordan now it will probably have to wait till tomorrow. I want to tell him why he's going to have a psychiatrist and dermatologist and God knows who else arriving in his room…'

'I wasn't complaining,' Louise insisted. 'I don't mind at all.'

'Good,' Daniel clipped, but he was clearly not impressed.

And who could blame him? Louise reasoned as she walked with him to Jordan's room. The Louise he'd worked with in London wouldn't have rolled her eyes at missing out on first lunch—she would probably have been paging *him* by now to come and explain things to the patient. But times had changed since then, Louise reasoned again, and, anyway, what would a man like Daniel know about breast-feeding?

'Hello Jordan.' Less austere out of his suit and without his entourage surrounding him, Daniel closed the door behind him and in a surprising move for such a usually emotionally abstinent man he sat on the edge of his patient's bed and attempted to make eye contact. 'I know things are rough for you at the moment...' Jordan's rather derisive sigh told all present that clearly he *didn't* know, and Daniel paused for a moment before continuing. 'OK, I've no idea what you're going through—but I do know some of what you're feeling.'

'Sure!' It was barely audible, but Jordan's single word dripped with sarcasm. The nurse in Louise wanted to intervene, wanted to tell Jordan that Daniel was just trying to be kind, but it would seem Daniel didn't need any help—taking absolutely no offence and instead moving straight to the difficult point with a skilful directness Louise could only admire.

'I'm concerned that you're shutting yourself off from everyone. Why don't you want your friends to come and see you?' When Jordan didn't answer, Daniel did it for him. 'Because of how you look?' Still Jordan didn't answer, but from the set of his face Daniel was clearly on the right track. 'You know this is only temporary? Your hair's going to grow back and in a couple of weeks you'll have some cosmetic work done to the scars on your face...'

'I've explained that to Jordan,' Louise volunteered as the stone wall of silence from Jordan remained. 'I also told him that a dermatologist was coming to see him about his acne.'

'Did you use anything for it before your accident?'

A tiny nod was his only response.

'Vitamin A cream,' Louise answered for him. 'Jordan told me that after the ward round.'

Vitamin A cream sounded a lot gentler than it was—by prescription only, it dried out the skin to such an extent it gave the recipient a mini-peel, but it was an extremely effective treatment for acne.

'Good.' Daniel nodded. 'We'll get straight onto it. You know there won't be much improvement for a couple of weeks, but it will settle. What we also need to work on is building you up a bit. You've lost a lot of weight and you've also got a lot of muscle wastage. Once you start exercising, that will come back, but in order to exercise you need to eat more. We need to get some calories into you and a lot of protein to help build you up—we can give you all the supplements but you need to do a lot for yourself, Jordan. You need to be exercising and getting into a different frame of mind if you want to see a rapid improvement.' He picked up a photo from the bedside and stared at the good-looking blonde guy for a long time before carrying on. 'Don't hide yourself away from your friends, Jordan.'

'Wouldn't you?' It was the first time Jordan had engaged Daniel, and even if it was faint and breathless it was a question nonetheless and Daniel pondered for a long moment before answering.

'Yes!' Daniel answered, and Louise found she was chewing on her lip at his rather too honest answer. 'But I know now that it was the wrong thing to do.'

'Now?' It was Louise talking, forgetting where she was for a moment, forgetting that there was a patient between them, her forehead furrowing into a frown at Daniel's choice of words.

'I mean,' Daniel answered crisply, shooting her an irritated look for the interruption, 'that I now know it *would* be the wrong thing to do—is that more grammatically correct for you, Sister?'

His sarcasm stung and Louise flushed, annoyed at herself for interrupting this difficult conversation but also confused, sure that Daniel's original words hadn't been a mistake. Daniel really did seem to understand some of what Jordan was going through and as he carried on talking that gut feeling was affirmed as he reached out to Jordan in a way none of the other staff had been able to. 'You need them, Jordan,' Daniel said gently but firmly. 'I know you feel embarrassed and over-whelmed now, and it might seem easier just to close the door and not face anyone, but now more than ever you need people fighting in your corner with you. Your friends will bolster you, give you a taste of the outside world, keep you up to date with everything that's happening out there…'

Louise watched as Jordan actually turned his head, actually managed eye contact, as somehow Daniel reached him. She could only marvel at it because, despite her cajoling, despite her best attempts to reach her patient, Daniel had achieved in a matter of minutes what she hadn't been able to. There was no jealousy, only admiration, and something else, too. Tears pricked her eyes as Daniel continued to speak to the young man, sounding as if he actually *did* understand what he was going through. 'The good thing about hitting rock bottom is that the only way is up. Let your friends share it with you—you're going to have a lot of things to be proud of over the coming weeks and months, you're going to achieve so much. If people don't see you then they're not going to really understand all that you've been through, so let them in, let them see you in the bad times so they can really share the good.'

'I will look better?' Despite Jordan's whisper, the fear in his voice spoke volumes.

'You couldn't look worse!' Daniel grinned and Louise caught her breath, wondering if Daniel had gone too far, but amazingly Jordan managed a small smile back. 'You're going to look great, Jordan,' Daniel said firmly, 'and that's not an empty promise. Yep, you'll have some scars but, hey, it'll add a bit of mystery. But the quicker you get eating and working out, the sooner you'll see an improvement. I'm going to get the psychiatrist to talk to you…' As Jordan shook his head, his body language the most animated Louise had ever seen it, Daniel pushed on, driving home the need for help. 'And I want you to talk to him or her, really talk. You woke up recently to find out that not only have you been unconscious for weeks but that suddenly everything in your life has changed. Everything,' he reiterated. 'And you need help to deal with that, just as anyone would. They might prescribe a short course of anti-depressants and if that's the case then I'd encourage you to take them. Take all the help you can, and then it's up to you do the rest yourself!'

'What about…?' the young man started coughing. Too weak to get the words out, he scribbled a few words on the whiteboard. Daniel read them and looked directly at Jordan, who was now avoiding his eyes.

'Do you mean will he address your lifestyle before the accident?'

Jordan gave a small embarrassed nod.

'That's up to you. You'll get out of counselling what you put into it, but given that you've been given a second chance at life maybe now might be a good time to make some lifestyle changes. But that's entirely your choice. I'm certainly not here to give you a lecture.'

'Thanks.' Jordan didn't manage to get the word out—he mouthed it—but Louise knew that Daniel's words had hit their mark. That was confirmed when a knock on the door heralded the arrival of lunch and Daniel picked up the stainless-steel lid and stared down at the unappetising mushy pile of food.

'Try your best,' he said, 'and if you can't manage that, then have mashed banana or an ice cream or something. But you have to try.'

And try he did. After just a short hesitation, Jordan poured out his fortified milk drink for himself and then, without prompting, picked up his fork to start eating the minced chicken and mashed potato. Even if it was just a small start, it was a good one, but the smile on Louise's face as she met Daniel's eyes rapidly faded, horror drenching her as she felt a familiar tingle in her breasts and a telltale cold patch spreading across her blouse. Embarrassed and feeling horribly, horribly exposed, she watched as Daniel's smile faded to one of confusion, until his knowing eyes finally took in what was happening. Louise, bright red with humiliation, folded her arms across her chest and practically ran for the door.

'Louise,' he called out down the corridor, but she wasn't listening, just grateful that he couldn't follow her as he would have to excuse himself first to Jordan, grateful that most of the staff were in handover now, and that she could make it to the staff changing room without anyone else seeing her.

Ripping off her soaked blouse, she grabbed a theatre top from the bench and put it on, embarrassed tears coursing down her flaming cheeks as she attempted to dry her bra under the hand dryer, appalled not just at what had happened but that it happened in front of him, that Daniel had had to be the one to witness this excruciatingly embarrassing incident.

'Louise.' His sharp rap at the door just made things worse. 'I've bought you a theatre top.'

'I've got one,' she called back, her thick voice not managing to cover up her tears. She watched the handle move on the communal change-room door, knowing he was coming in but desperate not see him. 'Just go away, Daniel.

'Please,' she added, ignoring Daniel as he strode in, turning her red, tear-streaked face away from him, concentrating on drying the ugliest maternity bra in the history of the universe and wondering what on earth she'd done to deserve this horrible moment. 'Will you just leave me alone?'

'Please, don't be embarrassed, Louise,' Daniel wasn't going anywhere—in fact, he was coming over. Her whole body cringed with mortification as he stepped right into her personal space. 'This is me, remember, not someone you don't know.'

'It's because it *is* you,' Louise gulped.

'Hey, I'm the guy who this time last week was lying, legs in stirrups, on a theatre table, who had the entire hospital discussing…' He didn't elaborate, but he did manage to drag out a tiny shiver of a smile. 'I'm sorry, I'm sorry, I'm sorry,' he said, pulling her into his arms, which was the first and last place she wanted to be. 'I should have just let you go to lunch. It never even entered my head that you needed to go and feed Declan.'

He was holding her, and no matter what way she tried to look at it, by no stretch of the imagination was he holding her as a colleague. His head was buried in her hair, his strong arms wrapped around her as he tried to goad her out of her embarrassment. It hurt, actually hurt, to be held by him, to glimpse all she had lost, all the moments in time he had ripped away from them, his arms a dangerous place to be.

So why did it feel like the safest place? Louise wondered as she gave in and leant on him, allowed him to soothe away her discomfort, allowed herself to lean on him for just this little while. Why, after months and months of hell, when Daniel Ashwood had been the source of her pain, the sole reason for the spinning mess her life was in now, did it all melt into insignificance the moment he held her?

'You're making things worse,' she attempted, feebly trying and gladly failing to push him off.

'What does that mean?' Daniel asked, and something in his voice unsettled and angered her. He truly didn't seem to know just how difficult this was, that the attraction was still there for her, hadn't for a single second gone away.

How could he not *know* how lonely it felt to be held in his arms and not be able to have all of him?

But maybe he did know, Louise thought as he pulled back just enough to look down at her, because the eyes that were holding her now seemed just as confused and bewildered as her own, his voice for once hesitant when it finally came. 'We need to talk, Louise.'

'To say what exactly?' A jolt of unease ripped through her—that now might be the moment for confession, for the truth that was so obvious to finally come out.

'Why do you think I'm here?' Daniel asked. 'Louise, why do you think I came here?'

'Because I was upset, because—'

'I wasn't talking about the locker room!' He let out a low, mirthless laugh, shook his head as if she'd spoken a foreign language. 'Louise—we can't talk here. Why don't we go out tonight? Just for a drink, to talk.'

'No.' In one self-preserving movement she pushed him

away, unable to tolerate the intimacy a moment longer. The pain he had caused was too recent and too raw to be obliterated by a tender moment in a locker room. A *drink* with Daniel Ashwood was the last thing she needed right now. She wasn't going to play along with whatever game he was leading her to this time. She had other responsibilities now—Declan to think of. She had just clawed her way back from the pit of despair Daniel had so readily thrown her into, but he wasn't letting her go anywhere, his hands capturing hers and holding them tightly.

'Yes,' he said, 'because I sure as hell can't go on like this, Louise, and I don't think you can either.'

CHAPTER FIVE

'SO THIS is your baby?'

Horribly awkward in jeans that felt way too tight and the most hurried make-up job in history, devoid of perfume because she hadn't been able to find it, Louise carefully placed Declan in his car seat on the floor before taking her seat at the table, grateful that Daniel was already there and she didn't have to sit in the bar in a high state of anxiety, attempting to feign nonchalance till he arrived.

'Maggie was out,' Louise explained as best she could with a mouth that was impossibly dry. 'I hope you don't mind me bringing him.'

'Of course not. He's gorgeous, Louise.' Daniel peered down at the sleeping baby and Louise held her breath, wondering *how* he couldn't see the resemblance, how his face wasn't breaking into a look of stunned recognition as he unwittingly glimpsed his son for the first time. 'He looks like you.'

And you!

'Do you want something to eat?' Daniel offered, his voice a touch stilted, and Louise realised that, despite his cool, suited appearance, he was as nervous as her.

'I really don't have time,' Louise answered honestly. 'He's

due to be fed in an hour or so.' She watched as his eyes flicked across the room to another table, where the epitome of Mother Earth was chatting, eating and laughing as a very relaxed baby consumed her dinner. She knew Daniel thought she was making excuses, knew that she had to set the record very straight here, let him know how it really was for her now, let him glimpse the reality of parenting before he even tried to step in.

'Declan's got no manners,' Louise said with a dry smile in her voice. 'Either that or I'm just not very good at it—it's more naked from the waist up on the couch than discreet feeding in a bar at the moment.'

He blushed—actually blushed. Oh, there was no whoosh of scarlet on that dignified face, but there was certainly a hint of pink on his sculpted cheeks as he asked what she'd like to drink.

'Just an orange juice, please.'

'Sure. You know I'm on call, that if I'm paged I might have to go…'

'Daniel!' She halted him with a single word, their eyes meeting for the first time since she'd sat down—as if she didn't know how things worked, as if he had to tell her how the night might end. They'd had many nights shattered by his pager in the past—that much hadn't changed at least.

She watched his back as he stood at the bar, ordering their drinks, a smile flicking across her face as he picked them up then almost instantly put them down and selected a straw for her—remembering one of the many little details that when put together had once made them a couple.

'Thanks.'

'Cheers!'

'How was Jordan after lunch?'

'A bit better,' Louise said, which killed that conversation stone dead.

God, it was awful, sitting in a bar making stilted awkward conversation when it had once flowed so easily between them, but by the time she was sucking the ice from her orange juice and had declined a packet of nuts twice, finally he opened up a touch.

'I've no idea what to say.' He gave a rueful grin, and the loaded atmosphere lightened a touch, his honesty at the awkwardness of the situation a welcome relief.

'You said we had a lot to talk about.' Louise gave her own rueful smile. 'Then again, talking never was one of your strong points.'

'Louise, we talked all the time.'

'No, Daniel, we didn't,' Louise said softly, in a non-argumentative tone. 'I talked and you listened.'

'That's not true,' Daniel insisted.

'But it is,' Louise affirmed. 'Sure, we talked about our day and about us, but I was going over things and I can see now that for the most part I was the one always opening up, telling you things about my friends, my family, my life before you.' She looked at him through narrowed eyes. 'What did you mean today when you said to Jordan that you know it was the wrong thing to do?'

'That has absolutely nothing to do with this.'

'It has *everything* to do with this.' Anger crept in then, her hand tightening around the glass as she spoke, tempted to slam it onto the table, as if somehow the noise, the gesture might break down the invisible wall he always had and still was putting up. 'Because it's another example of how little I know you, how one-sided our—for want of a word—*relationship* really was!'

'So you weren't happy?'

'I was very happy,' Louise countered, watching the confusion in his eyes at her answer. 'I thought in time you'd tell me, figured that when you were ready to, you'd open up a bit more, that it was just your way—only you ended it before we got there.'

'I was always open with you.'

'You've never been open with me, Daniel.' The woman she was now stared back at him, a year's worth of hindsight a wonderful thing as she faced this most difficult conversation. 'You were wonderful and loving and incredibly supportive, but at some point you'd made up your mind to end it, at some point it was over for us, yet you never hinted at a problem— you never considered telling me until the very end.'

'It wasn't like that!' For once he was uncomfortable, the suave, arrogant man fading a touch as he looked away and fiddled with the neck of his shirt while his other hand swirled the ice in his empty glass. 'Louise, I made a mistake that night— perhaps the biggest mistake of my life—and I realised it almost the moment you left. You didn't exactly give me a chance to apologise, you were practically on the next flight home.'

'Because you hurt me, Daniel.'

'You're the reason I'm here.' Finally he managed to look at her, no doubt taking in the shocked expression on her face but thankfully not commenting. 'Believe me, I wasn't in the market for a sea-change, Louise. I loved my job in London— you know that as well as I do—but after you'd left it held no appeal. I realised what I'd thrown away…'

'So why didn't you look me up?' Louise croaked, stunned by his admission. 'You've been in the country all this time and you never even thought to contact me.'

'It was *all* I thought about,' Daniel answered. 'But I wanted to be settled, wanted to find somewhere decent to live—which I have now.' He raked a hand through his hair and blew out a long breath. 'I suppose I was putting it off—I didn't know what to say, didn't know how you'd react.' His eyes met hers then and she flinched at the agony she witnessed in them. 'And I didn't know you'd have a baby. That, unlike me, you would have moved on.'

'You don't move on when you have a baby, Daniel.' She spoke very slowly, very clearly, because it was imperative that this much he understood. 'Your entire existence revolves around getting through the day. I'm up at five-thirty to feed and dress him—that's before I've had a coffee or a shower and packed his bags for a day in the crèche. Then I start work—'

'I get the picture.'

'No, Daniel, you don't,' Louise insisted. 'I thought I knew, or at least had some idea, but until you've got that little person in your life, you've no idea how much it consumes you, the sheer responsibility it entails.'

'I don't know,' he admitted. 'Perhaps more than most, because I've *never* envisaged having children, Louise—till now.' His voice was raw, appealing for her to understand with his eyes, to not interrupt, to let him say what he had to. 'It's just never been a part of my future and I still don't know if it's what I want. I don't know if I want to raise another man's child…'

And the easiest thing in the world would have been to tell him, to tell this man that not for a moment had she moved on, not for a single second had she left him behind. But it was perhaps the most dangerous thing she could do. If she told him now, told Daniel that Declan was actually his, then things would change for ever. The last thing she wanted was to be tied to Daniel for ever in child maintenance and visitation rights, arguments and hostility. The only tie Louise wanted binding her was love.

'I never get a full week off.'

'Sorry?' She frowned.

'Normally, I've got some work to do in that time, or a project I've been putting off, but for the first time in the longest time I've been lying on the sofa—only in my case it was naked from the waist down...' He gave a tiny smile of triumph as he lobbed the joke back and Louise gave a little blush of her own. 'Thinking,' he said softly. 'Thinking about you, thinking about us, thinking about him...' He stared down at Declan, who was stirring now, his little nose sniffing the unfamiliar air. Louise knew that the clock was ticking, that she had only five, maybe ten minutes to deal with the most important conversation of her life. 'What if we start again?'

'Start again?' She was popping Declan's thumb in his mouth, trying to buy them both just a little more time, trying to think of a suitable answer to the question she knew was coming.

'Take things slowly, I don't know, go out on dates, get to know each other—really get to know each other—and see where it leads.'

Let him in again.

'And what if it doesn't work?' Louise asked. 'What if you again suddenly decide that we're not what you want? I've got a baby now, Daniel. It's not fair on him to bring people into his life who might just walk out and leave.'

'I admit I don't know much about babies,' Daniel said, 'but we're not talking about a two-year-old here, Louise. If we can't make it work, if I can't accept...' His voice faded for a second, but he recovered quickly. 'Surely it's better to try now than in a couple of years—it isn't going to damage him.'

'Just his mother,' Louise responded heavily.

'You were right,' Daniel said, breaking into her jumbled thoughts. 'I haven't always said what I was thinking, what I'm feeling. What if I told you that I'd try? What if I told you that I will do my best to—'

'You can't even say it!' Surprising herself, Louise managed a tiny giggle and watched as a very reluctant smile ghosted his lips. 'I don't know,' she admitted. 'I don't know if I can risk being hurt by you all over again. I'd trust you with my life, Daniel, but I don't know if I can trust you with my heart.'

A loud bleep halted her and for once it wasn't Daniel's pager going off but Louise's mobile. Fishing in her bag, she pulled it out and glanced at the message on her screen.

HOW R U!!!! Dying to hear!

'Maggie,' Louise said.

'She's worried about you?'

She looked at him, looked right at him as she answered. 'Do you blame her?'

'Will you think about what I've said?'

'Of course.' Louise nodded, and clearly Daniel really had no idea how women's minds worked. As if he had to ask her to think about it! Didn't he realise that it was *all* she was going to be thinking about, that the obsessive, compulsive mind of a woman in love was already dissecting and analysing the content of the conversation and trying to come up with a very neat conclusion.

'I have to go.' She truly did. On cue, navy eyes peeped open, followed a tenth of a second later by a bellowing, hungry cry that demanded his mother's attention. He angrily spat out the tiny thumb Louise attempted to placate him with. Staring down at his sweet, innocent face, she simultaneously berated and was grateful for the fact he looked so much like his father, knew that for the rest of her life, with every smile, every flash of blue eyes, she'd be reminded of all she might lose if she didn't say yes to dating Daniel.

If she didn't load the gun and play a game of Russian roulette with her heart.

'Do you want me to carry—'

'My emotional baggage?' Louise attempted a joke, but her throat was thick with tears as with a mixture of strength and tenderness he easily picked up the car seat she usually struggled with and walked along the pavement beside her. And Louise knew with a stab of longing that to the world they must look like any other little family, out enjoying a balmy Melbourne evening. Worse, she thought as Daniel rather clumsily strapped the car seat in for her, they *were* another little family.

Just a very messed-up one.

Could she do it? Standing rigid on the kerb, she watched him check the straps, watched him smile at the tiny baby he was offering to try and love. And she knew that if for nothing other than Declan, she had to give this a try, had to put her heart on the line and try to trust this man all over again.

And if it worked, if Daniel really could prove that he'd changed, that he was someone she could trust, then she'd tell him the truth.

Despite the warm evening, Louise shivered at her monumental decision, drenched with panic as he calmly walked over to her.

'In the spirit of our new-found openness…' Daniel's hand reached up, stroked a strand of hair the wind had blown behind her ear and for a second longer let his finger graze her cheek. 'I should tell you that you look amazing tonight.'

'Next Thursday…' Not the most eloquent of responses, but as his eyes darted with hope she knew he understood. 'We'll have dinner—you bring the food!'

'*Next* Thursday?' Daniel checked, smiling but clearly bewildered, not because he'd been invited to dinner and told to bring the food—he knew from days of old that Louise never cooked! No, clearly he was confused as to the rather long time delay. But Louise just nodded. She certainly wasn't going to tell him that if she ate nothing, drank gallons of water, pilate'd, jogged and did a million sit-ups each night between now and then, she might *just* be ready to start dating! Jumping into her seat and clipping on her seat belt, she wound down the window before she finished her sentence. 'You can come over for dinner *next* Thursday.'

CHAPTER SIX

IT WAS actually *nice* to be back nursing and doing the job she had always loved.

Nice to feel her confidence returning, nice that even on a mere thousand calories a day, the hormone-riddled, labile brain she'd been left with after giving birth was actually capable of making decisions, working out drug doses and being able to chat with a patient all at the same time.

Nice to see Daniel every day, Louise reluctantly admitted, trying and failing not to notice how divine he looked as he raced onto the ward between cases to check on one of his post-operative patients that Louise was extremely concerned about. Dressed in theatre gear, a blue cap tied onto his head, he looked exhausted, concerned and irritated all at the same time.

And also impossibly handsome!

Edward Hamilton had been sent to the ward directly from Theatre following a motor vehicle accident, which meant that the recovery ward had been the first time Louise had met the patient. In a prolonged operation, 'Dan The Man', as the theatre nurse had jarringly called him, had repaired a nasty laceration on his liver. A splenic haematoma had been noted, but Daniel had chosen not to remove the spleen, instead ordering strict observation. Which would have been a hard ask, Louise knew that. There was some chance of the spleen rupturing, not just immediately post-op but over the next couple of months, and Mr Hamilton would be told when he was well enough not to travel too far off the beaten track for a while. If his spleen did end up rupturing, emergency surgery would be required.

There'd been nothing she'd been able to put her finger on when she'd called Daniel to request that he come and check the patient over between theatre cases. This had therefore made the call rather difficult, as she had been well aware that Daniel's theatre list was already way behind schedule because of the prolonged emergency surgery he had undertaken. But in the two hours since Mr Hamilton had been collected from Theatre, though his obs had remained relatively stable and the drains collecting excess fluids from his wound were well within normal limits, Louise didn't like the look of him, or, as she'd explained to a very disbelieving Elaine, she didn't like the colour of his tongue.

'His tongue!' Elaine gave her a very wide-eyed look.

'I saw it once on another patient—'

'You really expect me to ring Danny in the middle of surgery when all the patient's obs are OK and tell him that the agency RN looking after his patient doesn't like the colour of his tongue?'

'No,' Louise answered tartly. 'I'm more than capable of making my own phone calls, Elaine. And for the record,' she added, picking up the telephone and doing just that,

'I'm not from the agency—I'm employed by this hospital, just as you are.'

And no doubt Elaine would have given an equally smart retort but even before Louise had replaced the receiver, the blood-pressure machine alarm went off and, as was often the case on a busy surgical ward, an already busy afternoon became suddenly hectic in a race to save Edward Hamilton's life.

'What's happened?' Daniel arrived and didn't even glance over at her, his concern solely for the patient—and rightly so.

'Blood pressure's just dropped and the drains are filling.' Louise held up the two drains that were clipped to the edge of the bed—normally a few millilitres of haemoserous fluid could be expected but already the drains were full and needed to be emptied, which Louise was onto as Daniel palpated the patient's abdomen. He stopped as the pager that was clipped to his top started shrilling loudly, warning him he was needed for an emergency.

'Don't worry, that's me,' Louise said, as he let out a rapid curse, because even Dan the Man couldn't deal with two emergencies at once. 'I just had Emergency page you.'

'It is,' Daniel affirmed, still having to check his pager, just in case he was required elsewhere, then clipping it back on his top. 'Right, let's get some more blood from the lab,' he said. 'For now open the IV full bore—he should have another IV site.'

'Yep,' Louise said, because she'd already checked, running through some plasma expander before Daniel had even asked for it and connecting it to the other IV site, letting it run at the maximum rate to give Mr Hamilton the fluids he desperately needed.

'Let's get him straight to Theatre.'

Louise gave a relieved nod that it was Daniel who had come to do the review, Daniel who didn't ever waste time procrastinating before he made a decision. 'I'll have a quick word with his wife—can you grab me another consent form?'

'Sure.'

Mrs Hamilton was beside herself with worry. After hastily being asked to leave the area, she had hovered anxiously in the corridor, watching the hive of activity going on behind the curtains, and even though Theatre was what was desperately needed, Daniel took a brief moment to explain the situation to his wife. The difficult conversation had to take place in the corridor as there literally wasn't enough time to guide the shaking woman to a quiet room, and Louise stood with her as Daniel, in his clipped voice, explained the situation. And though sometimes she wished he could be more compassionate with patients and their relatives, there was something incredibly reassuring about Daniel's directness. Something in his demeanour that instilled confidence as he explained the facts and obtained the woman's consent for the further surgery.

'Do you think it's his spleen?' Mrs Hamilton's voice wavered as she read the hastily drawn-up consent form.

'Till I open him up I won't know,' Daniel said. 'As I explained, it could well be his liver that's hemorrhaging—the sooner I can stop the bleeding, the better chance he has.'

Louise's heart went out to the other woman as she shakily signed the form, her face as drained of colour as her husband's, her eyes disbelieving as she tried to fathom how, in a few short hours, her whole world had changed.

'Can I see him?' she choked. 'I won't be long, I just want to tell him…'

'Of course.' Daniel nodded, and only when she dashed off did he close his eyes for a moment and let out a worried sigh.

'I should have just taken it out—I was that close to doing it.' He held up his finger and thumb to show a tiny space. 'But it didn't look too bad and he was so unstable on the operating table—'

'You did what was right at the time,' Louise broke in. 'That's all you can do. So you do think it is his spleen?'

'I hope to God it is,' Daniel answered grimly. 'Because with the mess his liver was in and the trouble I had repairing it, if he's bleeding out there, I don't think there's going to be much more I can do.

'Let's go!'

Staff were everywhere, helping Louise with the many things that needed to be done in a few brief minutes—from running down to the lab to collect more precious blood for the patient to alerting the theatre that their earlier urgent case was about to reappear.

'Could you call the porters?' Louise called out as she transferred the oxygen from the wall outlet to a portable machine for the brisk walk to Theatre and collected some emergency supplies. Even though Theatre was only a few minutes away, if the patient collapsed en route he would need to be treated promptly and Louise had to be sure she had all the equipment she might require.

'We'll take him ourselves.' Daniel shook his head, clearly not prepared to wait for anyone, his foot already removing the brake from the bed and starting to wheel it away. Louise hastily grabbed Mr Hamilton's notes and X-rays.

'You go right on ahead, Danny, and scrub.' Elaine somehow managed to flirt and push the bed at the same time. 'We'll bring him straight round for you.'

He didn't bother with thanks, probably didn't even notice the flirty smile and batting of eyelashes, but Louise did.

And she didn't like it one bit.

'Thanks, ladies.' Clearly exhausted, Daniel appeared on the ward just as Louise was about to head to the crèche to pick up Declan and go home. His hair was damp and messy from a full day stuffed into a cap and there were dark shadows under his eyes and Louise knew that his day was nowhere near over. She'd already rung Theatre to check on Mr Hamilton, but apart from being told that the second lot of surgery had been particularly difficult and that he was now in Recovery, awaiting a bed on ICU, Louise wasn't much wiser as to what had happened and was genuinely pleased for professional reasons when Daniel managed a brief appearance to check on a different patient and update the ward. 'His spleen *had* ruptured. It was good that we got him to Theatre so quickly— it was a massive bleed...'

'Then it's lucky that *we* got him in time—' Elaine started, and though Louise could easily have pointed out that Elaine hadn't even wanted to call a doctor to review him, frankly she couldn't be bothered. And, anyway, it was Daniel who interrupted her.

'Luck had nothing to do with it,' he said firmly. 'It was entirely down to diligent nursing care. On paper, Mr Hamilton looked OK when Louise called. A lot of nurses would have waited—doctors, too,' he added, and Elaine at least had the grace to blush a little. 'You did very well, Louise—as always!'

Their eyes met and Louise coloured up, feeling that squirming pleasure of old—remembering the tiny secret smiles that had filled their working days in London, the double meanings in their conversations, the 'work calls' that had been anything but, glimpsing the pleasure that could soon be hers all over again.

'You look completely exhausted, Danny,' Elaine said, quickly recovering from her flash of guilt and going on to far more important matters! 'Would you like a coffee? Decent coffee,' she pushed boldly. 'I've got some in my locker!' 'Louise could only admire her boldness, well, only because she knew Daniel well enough to know that he'd turn Elaine down. A coffee and a flirt just wasn't his style—and Elaine was definitely flirting!

Famous last thoughts! Louise's head practically turned a full 360 degrees, as after only the briefest of hesitations, Daniel rewarded Elaine's efforts with a very nice, albeit tired, smile. 'Sounds good!'

CHAPTER SEVEN

'Wow!' Breezing into Jordan's room the following Thursday, Louise nearly dropped the cup of medicine she was carrying as she saw Jordan, who had long since become her favourite patient, instead of dozing after lunch, up on the treadmill, his skinny, wasted legs struggling to keep up with the slow pace, determination etched on his features.

'I'm sorry.' Turning around, Jordan gave an apologetic smile. 'I know I'm supposed to wait till there's someone in the room.'

'For now, you should let us know,' Louise said, 'but I'll speak to Mr Ashwood when he does his round tomorrow and tell him how well you're doing. I'm sure he'll be delighted with your progress—you're doing great!'

'So are you.' Jordan grinned at his favourite nurse. 'Have you lost weight or something?'

'A bit,' Louise gave a pleased, embarrassed shrug.

'And your hair, it's…' Jordan frowned as he peered more closely '…nice, sort of shiny.'

'I just used a different conditioner,' Louise said blithely, which was a rather paltry summing up for the high-gloss salon treatment and eyebrow wax that would appear on her credit-card statement at the end of the month!

'Danny's cool.' Gossip over and slightly breathless, Jordan stepped off the machine and Louise was thrilled that he didn't collapse on the bed. Instead, he moved to the chair and opened a can of high-protein drink. 'I was feeling so sorry for myself.' Jordan's voice was getting stronger and, unlike just a few days before when she'd had to strain to catch every breathless word, Louise was able to do his obs and tidy up his rather messy room while chatting to him, though the Daniel that Jordan was describing wasn't a particularly familiar one! In fact, the *Danny* Jordan was describing sounded like a different doctor entirely.

'He comes in to see me quite a lot—sometimes late, when he's finished operating.'

'That's nice,' Louise said, but she was frowning. 'How often?'

'Most days he comes in for a chat—tells me to keep at it. He told me that I should eat within half an hour of exercising if I want to start putting on some muscle. He said that when he….' His voice trailed off and Louise looked up from the pillows she was changing, checking that he was OK—now and then Jordan struggled to swallow, but from what she could see he was doing fine. In fact, Louise realised, he'd chosen to end the conversation.

'When he what?' Louise asked.

'Nothing.' Jordan shrugged, blushing a bit. 'It was just something he told me—made me realise that he understands.'

She had no idea what Jordan meant. Daniel was surely the last person who would understand how it felt to be a teenager. Louise had wondered sometimes if Daniel had bypassed adolescence and gone straight into serious adult mode, but, then again, hadn't it been *Danny* who'd reminded his team not to lose sight of the fact that Jordan was so young, to take his acne and depression over his body changes seriously?

But whatever the reason, Jordan had clearly became a rare favourite of Daniel's, and the fact he was taking some time out of his busy schedule to pay a bit of extra attention to this young patient was clearly reaping rewards. Jordan was more than a little impressed by his 'cool' doctor and was finally motivated.

'Right, if you can leave your cocktail for a moment,' Louise joked as she pulled on some gloves, 'can you lift your T-shirt so that I can put some cream on your back?'

His skin was still a mess. The cream and medication he had been started on would take a couple more weeks to start taking effect, as would the anti-depressants the psychiatrist had prescribed, but whatever Daniel had said to Jordan was clearly working. Gone was the sullen withdrawn young man. Visitors were coming in to see him now and just having his friends and a glimmer of confidence back was doing a thousand times more than any prescription ever could.

'How long do you think till I'm ready for rehab?'

'I don't know,' Louise admitted, as she rubbed in the cream. 'You've had a lot of tests done this week. Once Mr Ashwood's reviewed all the results, we'll know more.'

'Do you think I'll get rid of…?'

He still couldn't say it. He hated his colostomy so fiercely that Louise said the word for him.

'The colostomy is only temporary, Jordan. Depending on your test results, you'll either go to rehab and come back here for the surgery somewhere down the track, or if it's ready to be reversed then you'll have the surgery first and stay here in hospital for a bit longer. It'll take a good couple of weeks to recover enough to go to rehab.'

'I don't care,' Jordan sighed, as Louise pulled down his T-shirt. 'I just want rid of it.'

'You've got a call, Louise.' Shona popped her head around the door. 'And you've got some visitors, Jordan.'

A group of teenagers wandered in, offering 'yo's' and high fives, and seeing the expression on Jordan's face, Louise was only too happy to ignore the two-visitors rule and go and answer her call.

'Sister Andrews speaking.'

'God, you sound formal,' Maggie giggled. 'Just ringing to let you know I *definitely* won't be home tonight—I'm going out with a friend and intend to drink too much to drive home so I'll crash there.'

'There's really no need. It's not as if…' Louise started, but Daniel chose that moment to appear on the ward and, like moths to a flame, every nurse within sight chose to have to locate something at the nurses' station. So Louise was forced into silence as Maggie prattled happily on.

'There's *every* need. I loaded the dishwasher before I left and I've moved Declan's cot into my room!'

'Why?' Louise asked as Daniel gave her a brief nod and asked her if she knew where Jordan's obs chart was.

'I've got it here,' Louise said, handing it to him. 'I was just about to write it up.'

'That's him, isn't it?' Maggie squealed in delight down the phone, taking advantage of Louise's forced silence and talking ten to the dozen. 'Why do you think, Louise? For heaven's sake, it's hardly a conventional first date. And anyway you two never could keep your hands off each other!'

'Personal call?' Elaine asked before the receiver had even been replaced.

'Actually, no,' Louise answered sweetly. 'Just the NUM running by my shifts for Outpatients.'

'Outpatients?' Daniel actually looked up and frowned. 'Why on earth are you going to Outpatients?'

'Louise is just a *temporary* on the ward,' Elaine rapidly explained, then equally rapidly flicked her out of the conversation. 'So, to what do we owe the pleasure of a consultant on the ward this afternoon?'

'I want to go through all Jordan's notes and results—I'm going to discuss his case with a colleague tomorrow. I'm veering towards taking him back to Theatre for a colostomy reversal sooner rather than later.'

'He'll jump at the chance,' Louise said, even though from the scowl on Elaine's face she clearly thought Louise had no part in the conversation.

'Exactly.' Daniel nodded. 'That's why I want to be as sure as I can that we're likely to proceed before I say anything. Also...' This time he did turn to Elaine. 'I wanted to tell you about a probable admission.'

'So tell me!' she sparkled, and Louise smothered a giggle as Shona rolled her eyes.

'Amanda Bennett, with a UTI and query appendicitis. She's also thirty weeks pregnant, which is making the diagnosis rather more difficult.' It did. A women's anatomy changed during pregnancy, the growing baby shifting the appendix higher—and that, coupled with her urinary tract infection, was, as Daniel explained, making diagnosis all the more difficult. Certainly the last thing he wanted was to unnecessarily take a pregnant woman to Theatre for an operation. 'She's got some tenderness in her right loin—nephritis from the UTI—and she's febrile, but she's prone to urinary tract infections and the pain's different this time. I think it could be a bit of a red herring.'

'So what are you doing for her, Danny?' Elaine breathed, as Shona gagged over her paperwork.

'She's already had her first dose of antibiotics and we're rehydrating her. The obstetricians have seen her and the baby's fine. No sign of premature labour—though she is at risk—so the ball's been passed back to me. For now I'm going to watch her. Hopefully she'll be a new woman once the antibiotics kick in, otherwise I'm going to be taking her to Theatre.'

'So we're just to observe her for now,' Elaine said, crossing her neat skinny legs and writing it all down.

'Yep and keep her nil by mouth, at least till I see her in the morning. Just give her ice to suck for comfort.'

'Poor lady,' Elaine sighed. 'It must be scary for her.' It was Louise rolling her eyes now—if Elaine thought she'd win Daniel over that way, she was way off the mark. Emotions and medicine were two different spheres for him and Daniel just gave a shrug as he picked up Jordan's pile of notes, ready to head to the doctors' room. 'I mean, the fact she's pregnant and...' Elaine's voice petered out as the emotional desert again just shrugged.

'Oh, well, at least she's in the right place.'

'Can I bring you in a coffee?'

'No.' He didn't even add a 'Thanks' but, unperturbed Elaine pushed on. 'What time do they let you escape tonight, Danny?'

'God knows,' he answered, turning again to go. 'I'm on call.'

'Only, I'm on a late shift tonight. A few of the *regulars* on the ward are going to the pub for drinks later tonight...' And even if she'd been very pointedly excluded from this rather exclusive invite, it was the first Louise had heard of it—in fact, she could almost guarantee that Elaine was planning to be the only one there! 'You should join us.'

'I can't tonight,' Daniel said. For a tiny moment he caught Louise's eyes and she practically burst into flames as he ignited her with *that* look. 'I've got other plans.'

The second she arrived home—after first spending a small fortune at the deli and bottle shop—she deposited Declan on his play rug and, like a woman possessed, ripped through the tiny flat. Maggie's version of tidy seriously differed from hers and half an hour was spent locating coffee-mugs and wineglasses in the most unlikely of places. After feeding and changing Declan into his tiny pyjamas, the rather more mammoth task of transforming her postnatal body into something akin to its former glory began.

Lying in a full bath, wearing a hideous shower cap to protect her newly glossed locks, she took a shakily held razor to legs that hadn't seen one in months and exfoliated her skin before climbing out and critically eyeing herself in the mirror, wondering, not for the first time since Declan's arrival, just what the hell had happened to her body. The nubile, skinny one she'd owned before pregnancy had gone for ever—hadn't even returned to collect its deposit! Her once flat stomach, courtesy of living off two minute noodles the entire time in London, had vanished, now replaced with soft curves.

Continuing her critical examination, Louise turned around and eyed her rear in the mirror, instantly regretting it as she gazed at a rather dimply bottom not obliterated enough by the rapidly fogging up bathroom mirror. Sighing, she turned to wipe the glass, only for her attention to be caught by the two bits that had changed the most!

They were massive! It was the only word to describe them, not beach-babe massive, just huge milky white things that screamed of motherhood and made her feel as sexless as…well, her own mother.

She sat down on the edge of the bath, realising that she wasn't just keeping Daniel at arm's length because of the fear of getting hurt by him. There was a good dash of vanity splashed into the cocktail, too—wondering how he'd respond to the not-too-subtle changes in her, and wondering how she'd respond, too! God, she'd once been so confident with Daniel, had felt like some sort of goddess when they'd slept together. A tiny whisper of something desperately unfamiliar shivered through her as she recalled their love-making, the passion they had unleashed in each other, the places he had driven her to, the sheer unadulterated delight they had taken in each other's bodies.

'Surprise delivery!'

Maggie's cheerful rap on the bathroom door had her jumping out of her naked skin.

Muttering, Louise pulled on her robe and reluctantly opened the door, not wanting anyone to see her in this highly anxious state. 'You're supposed to be out for the night!' she growled, glowering at her flatmate.

'After I've given you these.' Maggie smiled sweetly, depositing a carrier bag in her hand.

'What's this? Louise asked, peering into the bag and almost passing out at the sight of some very tiny purple velvet triangles.

'An early birthday present.' Maggie grinned. 'And Christmas present, too—they cost a bloody fortune.'

'I'll look like a prostitute.' Louise could only laugh at Maggie's appalling taste, or lack of it, as she peered in the bag then held up a rather questionable-looking bra and G-string.

'You'll look like a yummy mummy!'

'I don't think I'd be able to get a leg through this, let alone my bottom—anyway, I have absolutely no intention of sleeping with him!'

'I know.' Maggie grinned. 'But I also know you're feeling fat, sexless and completely unlovable, and I read in a magazine that if you wear sexy underwear, just the *mere* knowledge of what's on underneath makes you feel more confident…' Maggie picked up one very large, very white maternity bra from the bathroom floor and, screwing up her nose, held it out as if was some 'off' meat she'd found at the back of the fridge. 'Surely it has to make you feel better than this! I'll go and bury it at the bottom of the laundry basket just in case he snoops.'

'I have no intention of sleeping with him—we're taking things slowly,' Louise said, running after her, but Maggie just laughed. 'I don't,' Louise insisted, but Maggie wasn't listening. Instead, she was rummaging in her handbag and pulling out a nearly empty bottle of Louise's missing perfume.

'That's mine!'

'I don't think so…' Maggie said, feigning innocence but handing it over after a few generous squirts. 'Sorry, I couldn't help myself.'

'It's nearly empty!' Louise wailed, having to tip the bottle to douse herself in her favourite scent. 'That was a full bottle you've used.'

'I'm going to miss this,' Maggie said, and if it was a diversion tactic it was a good one, because standing in the living room, arguing about stolen property and getting ready for a date, Louise was hit by such a wave of homesickness that she forgot to be cross with Maggie.

Homesick before she'd even arrived in her new house;

already missing the dramas of two single women sharing a flat; already missing the tears and giggles, even though it wasn't yet quite over.

'When do you pay the deposit for your new place?' Maggie asked, her voice strangely subdued.

'Tomorrow,' Louise answered. 'They've just got to check my references and then hopefully I should get the keys.'

'It's a lovely house,' Maggie said with forced cheerfulness. 'Small, but the garden's lovely and it's really close to the beach.'

'You sound like the real estate agent.' Louise gave a watery smile. 'Have you found someone else to move in?'

'Not yet. To tell the truth I haven't even started looking. I know it won't be a problem—there's always a nurse needing a room. I wish you could stay, though…' Maggie trailed off. They both knew it wasn't going to happen.

'So you're going out tonight?' Louise forced a smile, and closed the subject.

'Yep.' Maggie nodded. 'To the movies, and then I'm heading back to Glynn's to discuss the meaning of life…'

'Glynn?' Louise checked. 'I thought you weren't going to see him again after last time. Is this a date?'

'Hope so,' Maggie groaned. 'Right, see you later!'

'You're to come back home if it doesn't work out and forget about flatmate dating rules,' called Louise, as her friend went out the front door. 'Don't you dare stay out because of me!'

Oh, God, what to wear?

Without even looking in her wardrobe, Louise knew her choice was strictly limited—having refused to buy anything gorgeous until she'd got back to her pre-baby weight, most of the clothes she could fit into were suitable *only* for a night home alone, which left her with jeans that he'd seen her in or leggings which he certainly shouldn't! Still, a dash of purple velvet had surprising results because, eyeing herself in the mirror, Louise couldn't help but be pleased with the effect. OK, she didn't feel sexy, but sort of bordering on it. Maybe Maggie was right. Maybe a very little bit of purple velvet was what she needed to boost her sagging body and confidence!

But even with meticulous planning and ten days' notice, every carefully laid plan flew out of the window when Declan chose to break his newly established routine and wake up screaming. Pulling her very short, rather tatty dressing-gown back on, Louise flew into Maggie's room and tried to soothe him, popping his thumb in his mouth and stroking his forehead, trying every blessed trick she knew to get him back to sleep. It was all to absolutely no avail, until, with the clock ticking down on Daniel's arrival, she gave Declan the one thing he clearly wanted, even managing a giggle as at first attempt he spat out one newly moisturised 'delicately fragranced' nipple.

'It's still me, little man,' Louise whispered, forgetting about her impending date, cuddling him, marvelling at him, still, after three months, utterly stunned that she'd created something so amazingly perfect, and utterly stunned at how much time he took up! She'd *just* got him to sleep when a loud burst on the doorbell had them both jumping, but thankfully Declan only stirred and then drifted straight back to sleep. Aware of her lack of attire, Louise was sorely tempted to let Daniel ring the bell again so she could quickly pull on her jeans and a T-shirt, but, at the risk of waking Declan, instead she hurried down the tiny hallway.

'Daniel!' Blushing to her glossy roots, she opened the door and… He looked stunning. Daniel always looked stunning,

Louise reminded herself, but tonight he was dressed in black jeans and a black jumper, just the silver buckle of his belt breaking up the gorgeous lean line. The dark shadow on his chin was way past a five o'clock shadow and his hair was just the way she liked it—not as immaculate as he wore it for work, sort of tousled and messy, and it was like glimpsing again the man she'd said goodbye to just over a year ago.

'Sorry.' Daniel grinned. 'Did I wake you?'

'Yep.' Louise carried on the joke and gestured him inside. 'I was just relaxing with a book, waiting for my toenails to dry, and then fell asleep on the couch!'

'Where's the baby?' Daniel asked, peering around the rather tiny living room. 'I mean Declan.'

'Asleep,' Louise responded. 'He usually goes down around six-thirty, but he woke up just before you got here—hence the dressing gown.'

'I bought some pizza and a bottle of wine.' He held it out to her. 'Not for me—I'm on call…'

'So am I,' Louise said, shaking her head at the bottle. 'Twenty-four seven.'

'Well, what about pizza—are you allowed that?'

'Not according to my calorie count,' Louise answered, but it was softened with a slight smile. 'I'd love some, though.'

Seemingly brimming with confidence, he headed to her kitchen as Louise stood spinning in a vortex of confusion, wanting him here, wanting him to go. The only thing she knew for sure was that she didn't know how to react, as if all her usual responses were muted.

'Have you got a cutter?'

He was calling from the kitchen and attempting casual she walked in and pulled open the drawer.

'Here!' They both saw it at the same time, two hands moving towards the same object, a brief flare of contact, but as Daniel's hand moved away too quickly, she knew then, just *knew* he wasn't as assured as he was making out. Knew this was hard for him, too. She stared down at her hand, stared at where his had been, almost expecting her skin to redden, as if there should be some physical sign to justify the effect it had had.

And maybe pizza didn't sound like the most romantic of meals, but when he opened the box it smacked so much of *them* it bought tears to her eyes. He'd got *their* pizza, half margarita for her and half chilli beef mushrooms and onions for him—the same pizza they'd ordered a lifetime ago on the other side of the world.

'I'll go and get dressed.'

'Sure.' He was concentrating on cutting up the pizza but as she went to go he called her back. 'A bit like old times, isn't it?'

'A bit,' Louise admitted. 'A lot, perhaps.'

He turned enough to look at her. 'I miss it, Louise.'

'I know.' She did know. Having him there, not just in her flat but in her life, the tiny glow that burnt from just knowing he was around, being so very important in someone else's life—she missed it, too.

She never did get dressed. It was so very easy to slip back into ways of old when Daniel was around, half sitting, half lying on the sofa, eating dinner and talking about everything and nothing. And Daniel really was making an effort to be more open, because without prompting he told her about his parents' wedding anniversary and the fact his sister was expecting again—tiny snippets of information that most people divulged easily, only Daniel never had before.

'So you've found a nice place?' Daniel asked, when the

pizza was long since over and Louise felt full for the first time in ten days.

'Yep.' Louise nodded. 'It's just down the road. I'm signing the lease tomorrow.'

'What about Maggie?'

'She's staying here. We made a few noises about sharing the house, but at the end of the day it would have created more problems than solutions.'

'You'll miss her.'

'I'm getting used to missing things.' Louise shrugged, leaning forward and reaching for her drink, and that was the moment the talk that had come so easily faded. At the same moment he reached out to get it for her, his hand dusting her thigh as he stretched over her legs to reach it. Her dressing-gown gaped just a fraction, a fraction that between friends would go completely unnoticed but never between lovers.

'Louise…'

'Don't.'

She took a long gulp of her drink, tried to think of something witty and meaningless to say, but words utterly, utterly failed her. She wanted him, wanted him so much it was impossible to think. A massive white elephant was sitting on the sofa between them and both were struggling to deny it was there. Maybe she should just sleep with him, Louise thought, as neither of them spoke or moved. Maybe once they got *that* out of the way, they could breathe again, face their problems with clearer minds. And clearly this white elephant had exceptional hearing, because Daniel was asking the question that was screaming in her mind.

'I know we're going to take things slowly, but what does that mean exactly?'

'Just start over again—like we were before, only talking this time.'

'I think we can manage that…' Daniel gave a tense smile. 'When you say like before…' He gave a tiny swallow, his Adam's apple bobbing in his throat as he attempted to voice what was the only thing on their minds. 'What about—'

'I don't know,' Louise answered, too quickly, too shrilly, because her entire body was taut with tension, *burning* with awareness as his fingers inched their way towards her.

'Because I have to be honest here, Louise, slowly in that department is the bit I'm going to struggle with.'

She didn't say anything, couldn't say anything, because she could deny it all she liked but it was bit she was struggling with, too.

Was struggling with now.

Dating Daniel and not being with him was the equivalent to swimming a marathon and trying not to get wet.

'Is kissing OK?' Daniel's low voice reached her ears, twitching a smile on her tense face.

'I guess,' Louise answered, managing only the briefest of hesitations for Miss Manners' sake. 'I mean, if we're dating, I guess a kiss is…' She didn't get to finish because he was across the sofa in a second, wrapping his arms around her, holding her, his hand lifting her face to his.

'I've missed you,' he said, and maybe they weren't the three little words she'd always longed to hear him say, but they were three words that mirrored her own feelings. 'Can we try and make this work?'

'It's not that simple,' Louise croaked.

'Can't it be?'

Could it?

She dared to look at him—dared because if she was right, if the tension, the arousal she could feel in the heavy air she was trying to drag into her lungs was there in her eyes, then she knew she'd be lost again.

And she was.

The irises of his eyes were practically obliterated by dilated pupils—two dark pools that she fell into. His lips moved towards her trembling mouth and hushed it with the softest, gentlest, most tender of kisses, that beautiful, arrogant mouth softer now as it found hers, the breeze of his breath on her face as he closed in. A tiny nervous swallow, her throat tight, her body kindled with arousal, and as his lips met hers, the soft feel of his flesh on her mouth, the mingling of their breath, in his arms was the only place on earth she wanted to be, because his touch obliterated confusion—like the sun coming from behind a cloud, it dazzled her, blinded her to everything except the one truth that mattered at this moment.

She'd missed him so.

Missed this.

Missed the feelings of not just a man holding her but this man, his kiss almost chaste in its depth, as if just the contact was enough for him now, her eyes closing for the delicious seconds it lasted, a tiny grumble of protest welling within her as after a brief moment he pulled away.

'Is that slow enough?' His voice was low and husky, his breath warm on her cheek, his arms still holding her. She felt herself unravel in his arms, felt the knot of tension that permanently held her together slowly start to come undone.

'Maybe a bit too slow.'

He was kissing her again, his mouth more pressing this time, his tongue sliding between her softly parted lips, his hand gently but definitely pushing into the small of her back. It was as if he were touching her epicentre, rousing into life the lust that had lain dormant for so long now, stirring her desire with every skilful move of his tongue then wickedly pulling back, leaving it to Louise to make the next move.

'Way, way too slow,' Louise whispered, dangerously, provocatively, because, yes, there was so much to say, so, very, very much to say, but right now none of it mattered, none of it even computed, because his eyes were holding hers now, staring into her as if he was looking at her very soul, adoring her as only Daniel could.

God, she'd missed him, had missed the masculine scent of him, the cool, faint-making taste of him, the way his mouth caressed hers, the way his toned hard body pressed against hers, holding her in all the right places, his touch, his caress blissfully familiar and all the more intoxicating for it.

'Oh, Louise.' His mouth had left hers now, saying her name over and over as if he needed to hear it, moving across her face, his chin scratching, pulling at the soft skin on her cheek, one hand slipping behind her neck, under the soft curtain of her hair. He held her face steady as he devoured her, kissing her eyes, her temples, butterfly kisses that were hot with passion, and she reciprocated with submission, let her head rest in the cradle of his hand, her whole body singing a response as her ardour was inflamed.

His mouth moved down to the hollow of her throat, working the pulse spots that leapt against the moist, hard wedge of his circling tongue. Giddily she succumbed, her want as utterly as loaded as his because nothing he could do to her could be too quick or too soon, because she'd been waiting for this for ever. His free hand pulled at the belt of her robe and he did the strangest thing—but to her it made beautiful sense. He didn't pull away, didn't ravish her with his eyes. Instead, he folded her tighter into his space, gathered her to him till every wanton inch of her body was pressed against his—all of it. Hot, greedy kisses on her shoulder, Daniel pushed the robe further down, her breasts pressing into him, the cold buckle of his belt pressing into her stomach. But that wasn't what she needed, and she wriggled on the sofa till the glorious hard length of him rubbed against her heated spot, heavy denim straining to contain him. Her greedy hands tugged at his zip, wanting to free him, desperate for him to take her, right there—anywhere—it didn't matter. She just wanted that most intimate piece of him inside her.

'Steady…' With supreme control he slowed things down, pulling back just enough to halt the abandonment, but his resistance was futile, his eyes taking in her aroused, feminine shape, and Louise knew that to him she was beautiful, heard his thick moan of desire as he moved away just enough to glimpse her.

And no sexy underwear was required, because he was pulling at the fabric, freeing one ripe swollen breast and tasting her with his hot mouth, claiming her breasts as his again. Impatient fingers tore at her knickers and a tiny beat of fear gripped her, not at him—never at him.

But at her own body.

'I haven't since I had…' She didn't finish, yet immediately he understood. There was no need to finish a sentence because when they were together like this they were completely in tune—more one person than two.

'Neither have I, since I had surgery…' He smiled wickedly down at her, slowly, sensually, intimately—*that* smile that she could never explain to anyone, *that* smile that she knew was reserved solely for her.

'I'll be very gentle,' Louise whispered with a grin—because he brought out that side in her, bought out the funniest, sexiest, most wanton part of her. And as they drifted into the bedroom Louise knew it was going to be magical.

Knew because it was Daniel.

They'd always been at their closest when intimate, which sounded like a given—but it was so much more than that.

His passion for her was utterly unreserved—his love-making completely without inhibition—almost as if it was the one way he could truly express what he was feeling for her, make up for his emotional asceticism.

Sex his apology.

And over and over she had accepted it—because he made her dizzy with want.

Any trepidation was gone as he took off her robe, laid her on the bed and joined her, kissing her more tenderly now, allowing Louise to dictate the speed. She took the pleasure of taking her time—slowly undressing him, pulling off his jumper and welcoming back to her vision the body she had missed so.

The lean muscular lines of his torso, the clean, fragrant scent that was always him, he didn't even have to touch her to arouse her—it was Louise's turn now. Louise's turn to kneel astride him, to taste the nutmeg-coloured nipples. His hands in her hair, holding her as she worked sensually down, teasingly, slowly undoing the buckle of his belt, sliding down his zipper and pushing the last of his clothing down over his slender hips. And thankfully he helped with the last bit, because Louise was transfixed—her mind, her hands, her lips completely absorbed with the beautiful task in hand.

'Ouch!' Louise whispered as her fingers stroked the shaved area from his operation, then teasingly stroking the black silken curls as he grew in her hand. Bending her head, slowly, slowly, she kissed it all better, his moans of approval arousing her more, his hands in her hair intimately guiding her. If she could somehow have captured a moment and lived it for ever, this would be the one—this guarded, inaccessible man, letting her in, letting her hold him, lick him, taste him, calling her name while she adored him as only a lover could. And hearing his pleasure, feeling it with her mouth, was perhaps the best foreplay of all, because by the time he gently turned her and laid her down beneath him she was so deliciously moist, so heavy with want that fear didn't enter her mind—just a delicious rush as he entered a fraction, an overwhelming gratitude for the tenderness he displayed as he moved slowly within her, teasing her with playful, shallow stabs till it was Louise asking for more, her head thrashing on the pillow, calves lifting to his buttocks, lips begging him to go deeper. And he responded. How he responded!

His body slid against hers as he thrusted inside her, his mouth everywhere, hers tasting the salt of his skin, drowning in the delicious confusion of every sense being indulged. Nothing could have prolonged this moment. Her whole body was tightening as he delved deeper, his breathing more rapid now, delicious involuntary movements that yielded a heady rush as they reached glorious oblivion together.

'Oh, my.' Louise was lying in Daniel's arms, experiencing the first real moments of peace she had known in over a year, his fingers idly stroking her face as the world came back into focus. 'I thought having a baby was supposed to affect your sex life!'

'It has.' Daniel grinned at her. 'Spectacularly!' He bent his head and kissed each breast in turn. 'And these are fantastic.'

She let out a shocked laugh—adoring, *adoring* this side of him and so happy to welcome it back, loving the intimacy not just of the love-making but that dreamy time afterwards, when *nothing* could shatter the moment.

Except the bleep of his pager.

Groaning at the familiar intrusion, Louise flicked on the side light as Daniel, gloriously naked and utterly bold, strode around the room, searching for his jeans and locating his pager. He pressed the speed dial on his mobile as Louise blinked at her alarm clock, surprised to see it was only nine-thirty.

'Elaine, what are you doing, still working?' His question was pure politeness, given that the night staff should be the ones ringing now, but something inside Louise twisted as he spoke to her. 'Yep, thanks for letting me know. Tell Luke to page me if he's at all concerned—otherwise I'll be there within the hour.

'No,' he answered carefully, as Elaine apparently asked him again to meet them at the pub. 'I'm actually quite busy.'

'Mrs Bennett,' Daniel explained, putting down the telephone. 'Her pain's getting worse.'

'Are you going in?'

'Luke is,' Daniel answered. 'But I told Elaine to let me know if she didn't settle tonight.' Elaine had probably thrown a handful of drawing pins into the woman's bed to ensure she *didn't* settle, Louise thought nastily, then instantly regretted it. 'I don't think I should wait for Luke.' Daniel gave a regretful shrug. 'I'd rather check her myself.' Which was so him— he just couldn't delegate.

'Do you want a coffee,' Louise offered, 'before you go in?'

'I'm fine.'

Not quite as bold as Daniel, she wrapped the sheet around herself and hobbled across the room to her dressing-gown, the insecurities that had plagued her earlier starting to come back now as she tried to drop the sheet, pull on her robe and somehow not display an inch of flesh.

'What on earth are you doing?' Daniel smiled, clearly bemused by her sudden modesty, but Louise ignored it, tying the belt of her robe and wishing she could have back just a tenth of the confidence she'd found in his arms. 'I'll go and check Mrs Bennett and then, if it's not too late, I'll come back.' He was pulling on his shoes, buckling his belt and looking absolutely divine.

'Are you sure about the coffee?' Louise checked as he stood up to go. 'I've got some *decent* stuff!' And it was the most incredibly childish and petulant thing to say, but embarrassment and insecurity were a dangerous combination and even though instantly she regretted saying it, once out there was no taking the words back.

'Sorry?' He gave a frown of confusion then started to laugh. 'You're not talking about the other day with Elaine are you? I had a coffee with her, for goodness' sake!'

'She was flirting.'

'So?' She could hear his irritation. 'It doesn't mean that I was.'

'I know.' Raking a hand through her tousled hair, Louise tried to shrug it off, grateful when Declan, disturbed by a combination of phones, pagers and a hungry tummy, let out a telling wail.

Nice one, Louise! Berating herself, she padded down the hallway, furious with herself for being so petty yet knowing deep down what the problem was.

Petty was all they would ever be until she dealt with the real issue; knowing that this attempt at a relationship was pointless if it wasn't based on truth.

The real truth.

Pushing open Maggie's bedroom door, Louise stared at the tiny guy in his crib, watched his little face creasing in exasperation, his fists flailing as he blindly sought comfort.

And Declan wasn't the only one.

Picking him up, Louise buried her face in his soft, hair, felt the wetness of his cheek against hers, and knew she couldn't do it, couldn't deny her son his father, couldn't pretend that there wasn't a whole lot more between them than passion. Maybe now was the time to tell him. Now, when he *had* to go to the hospital, had time to digest the news before he reacted...

'Is he OK?'

Daniel was standing there in the semi-darkness, his profile silhouetted by the tiny nightlight Louise kept on. He came over and stared down at the babe nestling in her arms, making tiny snuffling noises, his hungry lips searching for comfort. Louise's eyes were doing the same, watching Daniel's unreadable expression for some reaction, some recognition, her voice shaky and tentative when finally it came.

'Daniel, there's something I need to tell you...'

Don't do this, Louise!

Daniel didn't say it, but his head was screaming it, warning her with his eyes to, please, not go there.

'He needs to be fed.' How he tried to keep his voice steady, light even, to pretend somehow that he hadn't heard her words. 'And I really ought to get to the hospital.'

'Daniel, please, there's something you really need to know.'

Please, don't do this!

It was the one thing he couldn't take—he didn't want to hear her lie to him, to try to fob him off with a story that he knew could never, ever be true.

'I'm trying to tell you something, Daniel!'

'Maybe I don't want to hear it.' His voice came out way too sharp and he struggled to right it. 'Look, I'm sorry you were upset about Elaine.' He was giving her an out again, trying to give her some time to think before she spoke, before she ruined things for ever.

'I'm not talking about Elaine! I'm talking about your son!'

'Louise, don't!' This time he did say it, the words shooting out like pistols, firing warning shots that she still ignored.

'What do you mean, don't?' Still she gnawed away, heaping lie upon lie, tears streaming down her cheeks, and if Daniel hadn't known that what she was implying couldn't possibly be true then he'd have believed her—her pain, her tears so convincing that for a moment he wavered, told himself that maybe she really did believe that Declan was his. 'You act as if you've no idea,' Louise rasped, every word angering him more, that she could look him in the eye and so blatantly lie. 'You're a doctor, for God's sake, do the maths! Did it never enter your head that Declan might be yours?'

'I'll tell you what entered my head…' Daniel struggled to keep his voice down, wrestled with a barrage of conflicting emotions, because even if she was lying, she was standing there, tousled and beautiful from their love-making, a tiny baby in her arms, holding to her breast the one thing he couldn't give her. 'That I'd be there for you, that I'd support you and that in time maybe I'd love him as my own.' He couldn't bring himself to look at the infant, couldn't allow himself to glimpse the dream that for him was never meant to be. 'And then you do this. My God, you have the temerity to question me over a cup of coffee with a colleague when you rolled out of my bed and into his.'

'His?' He saw a flash of anger in her eyes, the rigid motions of her body as she put the baby down in his cot and followed him to her bedroom, the bedroom where such a short while ago they'd found each other, demanding he explain as he dressed with lightning speed. 'There's never been anyone else since you.'

'Liar,' Daniel roared, letting out a bit of the anger he'd been keeping in now there was a wall between the baby and them. He picked up his keys and stormed down the hallway, but she grabbed the arm of his jumper as he wrenched open the door.

'There never was anyone else—my lousy taste in men was solely reserved for you!' She was pulling at his clothes, so utterly taut with rage that for a second Daniel thought she might slap him, couldn't quite believe that they were reduced to this.

'It's the twenty-first century, for heaven's sake Louise. You can't just choose who you think will make the better father. You can't just decide to pass him off as mine. There are tests…'

'Never!' He watched as the spitfire that had raged suddenly spluttered and died, the rasping tears replaced by shocked silence, her angry red face paling at his words. 'I'll never put him through a test.'

'Because you might not like the result?' Daniel sneered, and this time he pulled the door open unhindered, stepped out into the night air with bile rising in his throat.

'Because I don't need any proof.' His whole body stiffened as she called out into the darkness. 'And because I don't need you.'

It had been the most vile of vile confrontations and hearing the door slam for a second he wished he was stupid, wished he was one of those guys who could just take it without question, could believe her in the face of such appalling odds. His head was pounding, the rotten, filthy taste in his mouth was building as over and over he replayed the poisonous scene in his mind until, leaning against a tree, he threw up, too devastated to be embarrassed as an old man walking his dog tut-tutted as he wandered past.

'Bloody drunks,' the old man called out.

'I bloody wish,' Daniel murmured, as his pager shrilled in his pocket.

CHAPTER EIGHT

'SORRY.'

Slipping into a chair, Louise grimaced as she arrived a full fifteen minutes late for handover. 'Declan took for ever to settle, and…' Her voice trailed off. She'd already caused enough disturbance without telling the whole room about Declan's restless night, the difficult morning she'd had feeding and dressing him and his tears when she'd left him at the crèche.

No doubt he was picking up on his mother's misery. The second she'd closed the door on Daniel, Declan had started shrieking, and because she was a mum, because there was no choice but to tend to him, there had been no real time for self-indulgence, no real time to explore her own grief at what had just taken place. Just a sleepless night attempting to soothe her son, to reassure him that they were going to be OK—to tell him and herself that they didn't need Daniel Ashwood in their life to get by.

'Louise, can you take Mrs Bennett?' a very sparkly Elaine asked once handover had finished.

'The query appendicitis?' Louise checked, but her attempt at togetherness failed as she eyed her handover notes.

'Oh, that's right—you were late and missed the beginning of handover!' Ignoring the barb, Louise listened intently as Elaine filled her in. 'Mrs Bennett went to Theatre late last night, had an appendicectomy and was returned to the ward at three a.m. One of the midwives came down at five a.m. and did a CTG, which showed an irritable uterus but no signs of labour. I would imagine once Danny's seen her, he'll arrange her transfer to the maternity ward, however.'

'How are you this morning?' Louise asked, smiling down at the pale woman and wrapping a blood-pressure cuff around her arm as she chatted. 'You had a bit of a rough night, I hear.'

Mrs Bennett wasn't the only one. Daniel would barely have left her apartment before his pager would have gone off, and performing an appendicectomy on a heavily pregnant woman in the middle of the night wasn't exactly conducive to relaxation. As for Louise, she felt as if a train had hit her, both physically and mentally.

Still, Mrs Bennett was her priority right now, and checking her obs, Louise did her best to make sure her patient was comfortable.

'Is your husband coming in?' Louise asked, attempting conversation.

'He's got to get the other two off to school. Maybe then, I guess.' Amanda gave a tiny shrug. 'Or maybe he'll just go to work, though I thought he'd have called by now.' She gestured to the phone on her locker.

'He probably overslept.' Louise smiled. 'Given that he was here all night. He's probably racing around, trying to get the children organised for school. He'll ring soon.'

'We'll see.'

Louise frowned at her patient's rather flat response, but as a delicious waft of aftershave greeted her nostrils, she continued to frown for entirely different reasons. 'Good morning, Mrs Bennett.' Daniel's assured, silken tones filled the room.

Bristling with rancour, Louise handed him the notes, appalled that he could looked so damned together when she felt as if she was falling apart—though on closer inspection he wasn't quite as together as he'd first appeared. Despite a few thousand dollars' worth of suit and a tie that would cover her rent for a month, his eyes were bloodshot, his skin had a ghastly tinge to it and every muscle in his toned body screamed with tension.

'Can I see her chart?'

She handed it to him without contact and tried to smile reassuringly at her patient as he carefully checked Amanda's obs chart then gently examined her, placing his hand on her stomach for what seemed the longest time. And probably no one else would have even noticed, but because she'd worked with him, because she knew him so damned well, Louise knew he was worried.

'That's quite a strong contraction, Amanda.'

'It's not too bad…' The patient shook her head but Daniel remained unconvinced.

'You're on a lot of pethidine—you probably didn't feel most of it.' He glanced over at Louise. 'She wasn't having contractions when they did the CTG—I assume the midwife didn't do a PV?'

'What does that mean?' Amanda's anxious eyes darted from Daniel to Louise.

'An internal examination,' Louise explained. 'When the uterus is irritable, generally we try to leave things well alone.'

She looked back at Daniel. 'According to the notes, no, she hasn't had one, though I've only just come on and only just started to do her obs.'

'How long have you been having these contractions?' Daniel asked Amanda.

'I wouldn't call them contractions.' Amanda gave a small shrug. 'I think they're just Braxton-Hicks', you know, the practice ones you get…'

'I'm going to ring the obstetrician and get you transferred upstairs,' Daniel broke in, deciding, as he often did, that he knew best! 'The appendicectomy went well—it's the baby we need to watch now.'

'Did Harry ask about the baby?'

'Harry?' Daniel frowned as he turned to the door. 'Your husband? Yes, he was extremely concerned. I spoke to him at length after the operation—'

'I mean about the baby.' There was urgency in her eyes as she stared up at Daniel. 'Did he ask how the baby was?' And acting skills didn't get handed out with a medical degree because Daniel hesitated just a second too long before answering. 'He was very worried. I don't specifically remember what he asked. I just did my best to reassure him—'

'He doesn't care.' Amanda started to cry, a ball of emotion on the rumpled bed, such a contrast to the controlled, together doctor who stood at the doorway. 'I bet he wishes I'd just lost it…'

'Amanda.' Louise moved to soothe her, to comfort her. 'Please, don't upset yourself at the moment—you really need to try and get some rest.'

'He didn't even ask the doctor how the baby was!'

'People react differently. He's probably beside himself…'

'He thinks it isn't his!' And it was so painfully close to the bone Louise had to physically stop herself from wincing. She just stood there for a second, frozen, as Amanda sobbed into the tissues she was handing her. 'He thinks I had an affair...'

There was an appalling silence, Louise knowing she should say something and berating her lack of words.

'He says it can't be his.'

'Just try to rest and not upset yourself, Amanda.' Daniel's clipped, cool tones did nothing to help and Louise flashed angry eyes at him as Daniel finished his consultation. 'I'll arrange your transfer.'

'I'm going to be sick!' The door had barely closed on Daniel when Amanda's distressed voice filled the room. And even if she wasn't a midwife, Louise was a nurse through and through and knew, just *knew* what was coming next even before the patient said it. 'I think the baby's coming.'

One hand held the vomit bowl as the other pushed on the emergency bell and thankfully Daniel was the first to appear, along with Elaine.

'Call the labour ward,' Louise called to Elaine, her eyes giving an urgent wide-eyed look as Daniel pulled on some gloves. The austere doctor of before disappeared as he gently explained to Amanda that he was going to examine her. Though an internal examination was not usually performed when labour was trying to be prevented, from the expression on Daniel's face when he examined her, nothing was going to prevent this one.

'Tell them to bring everything down,' he briefly looked over at Louise's but she was already on it. *'Stat!'*

There was quiet order in the room as Elaine came in with a rarely used delivery pack, even though chaos was surely reigning outside—emergency pages going out to the obstetricians, midwives, anaesthetist and paediatrician, lifts being held open as a resuscitation cot was wheeled from Theatre through to the surgical unit, skilled people dropping whatever they were doing and racing to where they were needed more.

'Slowly, Amanda.' Daniel's voice was incredibly calm and gentle as he told her not to push. 'Just try and pant through the contraction.' Louise knew what he was doing, trying to control the very rapid delivery, the small soft head of a thirty-weeker, not up to a traumatic, rapid entrance. To prevent brain problems, it was vital that the delivery was as gentle and as controlled as possible. 'You're doing really well.'

'I want Harry here,' Amanda begged. 'Maybe if he sees his baby being born, he'll love it…'

'He doesn't have to be here to know…' Daniel said, and it was as if her heart was being pierced again—watching him so gentle, so tender, saying all the right things to a stranger that he couldn't say to her. 'Just pant now, Amanda—that's it.' The door swung open, the obstetrician racing in and gloving up, but there wasn't time for anyone to take over. The tiny life was already making an entrance, and instead he spoke to Daniel through the next few seconds, the room filling as Daniel skilfully handled the emergency. And it hurt, hurt to watch as he delivered the infant, as his strong, big hands skilfully bought the tiny life into the world.

'You've got a little boy,' Daniel said, because no one else had time to. Apart from him and Louise, everyone else was concentrating on the tiny infant now, placing him on the resuscitation cot, flicking his feet to stimulate breathing, suctioning his tiny grimacing mouth until the weakest, feeblest of cries came from the cot.

'Is he OK?' Amanda was calling out for answers, oblivious to the placenta Daniel was delivering, her mind completely on her tiny son.

'Nasal flaring,' the anaesthetist called to the team, ignoring Amanda's question, his mind completely focussed on the little life that hung in the balance. 'He's struggling. Let's get him upstairs.'

'We wanted a boy,' Amanda said. 'Maybe now he's got a son he'll—'

'Amanda!' A terrified, stunned face appeared at the door and Louise knew without introduction it was Harry, his exhausted eyes taking in the scene.

'We've got a son,' Amanda sobbed, as her husband took her in his arms and held her, his stunned expression belying the quiet strength he offered his wife.

'They're going to move him upstairs in just a moment or two,' Louise explained. 'To the neonatal unit. It's the best place for him.'

Just the tiniest glimpse of her son was all Amanda was given, a few seconds to stroke his pale cheek before he was whisked away, leaving the whole room in chaos, with wrappers and packets littering the floor as if some whirlwind had blasted in and gone. It was almost impossible to believe that just fifteen minutes ago it had seemed like another routine morning.

'Go with him, Harry,' Amanda pleaded. 'Go and see how he's doing. One of us should be there for him!'

'I want to stay here with you!' If he'd been pale before, Harry was white now, his face etched with tension, his eyes screwing closed as over and over Amanda urged him to go and look out for their son.

'Could I have a word, Harry?' Louise gestured him outside,

and when he followed she led the stunned man down to the relatives' room, waiting till he sat down before joining him. 'I know this has come as a shock. It was very rapid. There really wasn't time to let you know what was happening.' She paused, unsure of what to say because even if she wasn't a midwife, she was a parent and surely he should be asking, surely he should be desperate to know how his son was. Then the door opened and Daniel came in.

'I've just had a call from upstairs,' he told Harry. 'You can go up and see your son—'

'He isn't my son.' The words hissed out and Louise found herself staring at her fingers, lacing them between each other. 'Amanda insists that it is, but the only person she's fooling is herself.'

'You're sure of that?' Daniel asked, giving a brief nod as Harry gave a resigned one. 'Well, whatever the case, right now your wife has just been through surgery and labour and has a premature infant in the neonatal intensive care unit…'

'I can't see him.' Harry looked up at Daniel. 'Do you understand, Doc? I can't just be a fool. I had a vasectomy two years ago, for God's sake. What am I supposed to do here, just pretend he's mine, pretend to Amanda that I don't know? When we both know…'

'That I can't answer.' Daniel was direct but it was necessary. Added emotion or opinions were not needed when they already abounded, and Louise was for once grateful for his cool demeanour, a chance to catch her breath as Daniel faced the practicalities. 'My only concern is my patient and her welfare, Harry. Midwives are with her now and once she's ready to be moved I'll arrange her transfer to the maternity ward. I think your questions are going to have to wait a while before they can be answered—for now I want your wife to rest and if that means you stay in here for a while, then I'm sure the staff can bring you some coffee.'

'You had the tests?' Louise's voice seemed to be coming from a long way off, her usual confidence utterly eroded, this situation just too close to home to allow for complete professional detachment. And even if it was none of her business, even if Amanda Bennett wouldn't have been the first or last woman to have an affair and pass the child off as her husband's, somewhere deep inside Louise knew the other woman had been speaking the truth, and that gave her the impetus to probe.

'Louise,' Daniel snapped. 'I mean, Sister Andrews. I really think Mr Bennett has enough to deal with now. Perhaps you could arrange an outside telephone line for him and some coffee.'

'Did you have the tests after your vasectomy,' Louise asked again, utterly ignoring Daniel and staring at her patient's husband, who squirmed uncomfortably in his chair.

'I had the surgery, love.' Harry gave a nervous laugh. 'Believe me, I was there and it's not something you'd want to go through twice!'

'You're supposed to have two clear sperm counts post-vasectomy.' It was Daniel speaking now, Daniel addressing things as Louise let out a relieved breath, knowing that if she'd been wrong it could have made a terrible situation even worse. 'The doctor would have explained that to you. Did you have the tests?'

'No.' Harry shook his head. 'I didn't see the need…' He was speaking to thin air. Daniel had already left the room, only to return a minute later with a pathology request slip.

'Now?' Harry yelped.

'Could you show Harry the way to the path lab?' Daniel stared at the man. 'If he wants to be shown, that is!'

'Well done.' Daniel's face was pale when she returned to the ward, but a muscle was flickering in his cheek. 'How did you know? I mean, if you'd been wrong, you could have made things so much worse.'

'I guess I just believed her.' It was the closest she'd ever come to hate, staring into the face of the man she loved, a man who simply couldn't believe her.

'Louise?' The pain in his voice was urgent and for a second it startled her, because, no matter what, not once had she seen him anything other than together at work. 'Louise, can we—'

'Talk?' Incredulous, she finished his sentence for him. 'Go to hell, Daniel.'

'Louise, please.' It was Daniel flailing now, Daniel reaching for her arm and trying to call her back. 'I *have* to talk to you!'

'You're too late,' Louise flared. 'Twelve months too late!'

Her name was being called from two directions and even if she loathed Elaine, she was infinitely preferable to Daniel at the moment. As the senior nurse walked towards her, Louise was glad to turn her back on him and braced herself for a sharp few words, but for once they didn't come. Elaine's face was actually kind as she spoke to her. 'The crèche just called. Apparently Declan vomited before—'

'Oh!' Louise shook her head as if to clear it, pushing aside the fact that Daniel's arm was still on her, her only instinct to go to her son, but knowing she had to make the right noises, knowing that just because the crèche was in the hospital she couldn't just dash off. 'Look, the midwives are in with Mrs Bennett. Is it OK if I take an early coffee?'

'Louise…' Why was Elaine being so nice? Why was she still looking at her with that concerned expression? Panic started to flutter inside as the horrible pause went on. 'Declan isn't in the crèche. The staff were actually quite worried about him and they've taken him straight to Emergency. I think you ought to go…' Elaine's mouth was moving, words still coming out, but Louise couldn't hear them. It felt as if her head had been plunged underwater and was being held down, everything muted and distorted. Her only thought was to get to Declan. She shook off Daniel's hand, which was still on hers, and could feel her legs heavy as they pounded down the corridor, saw her tense white fingers as they slammed on the lift button to summon it.

'Louise.' Daniel was there beside her, his voice attempting reassurance, but she could hear the slight wobble in it as he took her trembling hand and held it as she continued to press the button. 'He'll be OK, the staff are probably just being overly…' He never got to finish because his pager was shrilling, the urgent voice of the switchboard operator demanding his attention.

'Mr Ashwood to Emergency. Paediatric emergency. Mr Ashwood to Emergency!'

'It doesn't mean it's him!' Daniel was holding her up, and she could see he was torn, wanting to comfort her, to help, yet knowing the only way he truly could be of use was to go.

'It is him.' Her teeth were chattering, her eyes wide and panicky, as she relived in that split second the piercing cries that had woken her up over and over in the night, the arching of his body as she'd handed him over to the crèche staff.

The lift doors slid open, but Daniel had already gone. Lifts out of bounds to staff in an emergency, he'd already taken the stairs. Thankfully Shona was there—Shona dashing towards her and instantly taking over, guiding her into the lift and pushing the ground-floor button, not saying a word as the lift bumped down to the ground floor, just offering support as they raced silently down to Emergency.

It *was* him.

As the black plastic doors pushed open, Louise just knew.

Knew because no one seemed surprised to see her, just that awful sympathetic smile that did nothing to reassure as someone took her arm and tried to guide her into the interview room, and in a fit of rage almost she shook whoever it was off. She wasn't going to sit in a room and wait. She just needed to see her baby.

Their baby.

As soon as she stepped inside the resuscitation area, as soon as she saw Daniel's stricken face, Louise knew for sure that he knew.

The truth had been there for him to see, but Daniel hadn't wanted to. The same long dark eyelashes, the same high cheekbones and the same long limbs, just so much smaller. He was his father's son. And only now could Daniel see it.

'Declan!' Louise's voice was a strangled sob as she saw her little boy.

How could it be him?

How could the beautiful, vibrant babe she had nursed just a few hours ago be lying there so lifeless and pale?

'What happened?'

A voice she didn't recognise began speaking. 'Apparently he was a bit irritable this morning in the crèche. Oh, I'm Karl Baker, by the way, the emergency consultant.' The man didn't attempt to shake her hand, just introduced himself as Louise stood there, trying to take it all in. 'He started to cry and a staff member was consoling him when he vomited—he vomited bile and in an infant that can be very serious. He collapsed and they raced him up to us. He picked up for a short while, but there's been a further episode…' Thankfully the consultant was explaining things slowly, talking to her not as a nurse but as a mum, gently walking her through the probable diagnosis. 'We think that Declan has intussusception.'

'No!' Louise shook her head, because if that's what was wrong then he was very sick indeed. If what they were saying was true, then her baby, her precious, tiny baby, was really sick, his bowel having telescoped in on itself and necrosing, cutting off vital circulation, rapidly causing his body to go into shock. And if Karl Baker was right, her perfect, beautiful baby was about to be taken to Theatre and cut open.

'He can't have that—not that! It's just a bug he's picked up. There's loads around…'

'He's got redcurrant-jelly stool,' Karl explained gently. And the diagnosis started to ram home, long-buried paediatric textbooks springing to mind, the redcurrant-jelly stool found on a PR examination practically enough to confirm the diagnosis, the blood and mucus telling the staff the damage that was being wreaked inside Declan's body as his bowel twisted in on itself. 'We're resuscitating him with fluids and oxygen at the moment, but we're going to have to get him up to Theatre very soon. Mr Ashwood is the surgeon on call—'

'No!' Daniel's voice was hoarse but firm. 'Mr Masterton is the best paediatric surgeon.'

'He's not on take today,' Karl corrected in dismissive businesslike tones, rightfully turning his attention back to Louise. But something in Daniel's voice must have alerted him. As an emergency consultant he was clearly used to the twists that developed in the lives he cared for, and in a delayed reaction he paused and turned again, professional courtesy, compassion and patience all offered in the brief words he uttered next.

'Danny? Would you prefer it if I paged Mr Masterton's team?'

'Not his team.' Daniel's eyes never moved from Declan, but his hands raked through his black hair and despite her own pain, so visible was his that somehow it reached her. 'John Masterton is to operate.'

Nursing was all Louise had ever done, all she professionally knew. She gave her best every day to the patients in her care, but only that day did she truly learn the true responsibility of her job, the utter trust that *had* to be placed in others sometimes, handing over the most precious piece of you to a face you didn't know and yet believing them when they said they'd take care of him as if he were their own.

That he was in the best hands.

'He's too little.' Her hand was trembling over the consent form, gagging at what she was being asked to agree to, that if it was deemed necessary a colostomy might be performed and any further measures the surgeons found necessary. 'He was fine this morning.'

'He needs this operation,' the registrar explained again as *again* she stalled at the final hurdle. 'Mr Masterton's scrubbing now…'

'Sign it, Louise.' Daniel's voice was sharp, and she turned to him, startled by the anger in his eyes. He stared defiantly back at her and, clearly not caring who the hell knew, he pulled a pen out of his pocket and clicked it on. 'Either you sign it or I will.'

'Only the next of kin can sign, Danny,' the registrar flustered, clearly confused, but shutting up when Daniel's grim voice overrode him.

'I'm well aware of that, thanks. Sign it, Louise, or if you don't want the responsibility, then hand it over here and I will.'

CHAPTER NINE

'YOU should have told me!'

Over and over he kept saying it, like some sort of mantra, pacing in the waiting area like a restless animal as Louise sat there shivering, watching her knees bob up and down. Maggie was sitting next to her, the perfect psychiatric nurse, not intervening, not remotely fazed by the raw, unbridled emotion, just quietly observing and occasionally reeling it in. As the minutes ticked by into hours, as Declan's operating time ominously increased, the tension that had simmered started to bubble to the boil. For the first couple of hours they had sat in relative silence, recriminations put on hold, all mental energy focussed on pulling their son through, catching each other's eyes now and then, then tearing them away.

Shona had gone back to the ward, replaced now by Maggie, and never had Louise been so pleased to see her, infinitely grateful for the support she offered. She brought endless cups of coffee, peeled tissue after tissue out of the box and handed them to Louise. Letting her rant, letting her cry and sometimes letting her sit in silence. Louise's swollen, bloodshot eyes stared from the clock to the door, willing someone to appear, someone to come and give her an update, to tell her that this nightmare was over, that her baby was going to be OK. But as they moved into the third hour, Daniel's patience had long since snapped. The emotions he had struggled so hard to keep in check kept bubbling to the fore and all Louise could do was dodge the bullets he aimed at her, guilt impinging on guilt as she realised the utter depth of his despair, understood, perhaps for the first time, just what she had denied him.

'I told you Declan was your son last night!' She didn't even look up. 'And you walked out—remember?'

'Last night!' He gave a black laugh, utterly devoid of humour. 'He's nearly four months old, for heaven's sake. This is like some warped before and after shot—and you've made me miss out on the bit in the middle! The Louise I knew, or the Louise I *thought* I knew, would have told me…' He looked up at her, a fresh wave of anger mixing with the devastation she could see in his eyes. 'For heaven's sake, Louise, because of you I could have operated on my own son!'

'No.' Louise shook her head. 'Daniel, I wouldn't have let you operate on him. I'd have spoken up. And I didn't tell you before because you dumped me, Daniel; you dumped me before I even knew that I was pregnant. If we couldn't make it when it was just us, how the hell were we supposed to make it with a baby?'

'I'd have supported him. I'd have—'

'You'd have done your duty and hated us both for it!' The venom in her voice shocked even her, and as Maggie pulled her back she slumped. She couldn't deal with this, couldn't take his accusations now, couldn't fight back when her baby was lying on some sterile operating table. But the gloves were off now, the bell ringing again as Daniel, utterly enraged, literally beside himself with grief, summoned her to the ring for another round. 'You wanted what I couldn't give.'

'Yes, I wanted you—and you always held back!'

'Guys!' One word from Maggie and they were back on their stools, catching their breath, but still the fight continued, the mental sparring going on and on.

'You wanted children,' Daniel attempted, but she wasn't having it.

'And you didn't.' Louise stared back at him, held his eyes for the first time since the previous night. 'You said a baby was the last thing you wanted.'

'Because I thought a baby was the last thing I could have.' Burying his face in his hands, he dragged in air. 'I can't have children, Louise.' Oh, God, there was such a good retort there, and if Maggie hadn't placed her hand on Louise's arm she'd have delivered it, would have sneered it right across the room, but instead somehow she contained it long enough for him to elaborate. 'I *thought* I couldn't have children.' He dragged his fingers through his hair again and gave an almost angry shake of his head. 'It wasn't till today, when you spoke to Harry Bennett, that I realised I'd just assumed.'

'You had a vasectomy?' Her voice was incredulous, the day getting worse and worse with each passing moment. Men had vasectomies when their families were complete. Was he really telling her there was an ex-Mrs Ashwood, a family with children that he hadn't even told her about, that he'd left in England to pursue whatever it was he was chasing here? But his answer, when it came, hurt her more than her wild imagination ever could—the simple truth and simple honesty tearing through her, lacerating her with regret and shards of understanding.

'I had cancer.'

Oh, God, oh, God.

Thankfully Maggie's hand was still on her arm as his deep voice filled the tiny room. Her touch still offered quiet strength and support as Louise heard the man she loved tell her his painful truth, but because of her lie by omission, because of the mess they'd somehow found themselves in, there was nothing, *nothing* she could do to comfort him as he revealed just a little of his pain. 'When I was studying I had…' There was a long pause before he continued. 'I had a lot of chemo-therapy and was told at the start that it would affect my fertility…' His voice trailed off and Louise waited for him to elaborate, to reveal just a bit more. But because it was Daniel, Louise realised it was all she was going to get—the blackest moment of his life, apart from this one, reduced to a couple of stilted sentences.

'Why didn't you tell me?'

'It was years ago,' came his flat response. 'It didn't seem relevant.'

'Not relevant?' Louise shook her head in disbelief. 'What on earth does that mean? We were together, Daniel. How on earth could you just skip over such a huge piece of you? Even now you're not telling me anything. What type of cancer did you have?'

'What on earth does that have to do with anything?'

And all she could do was stare, stare at a man who was prepared to give so little, her lips white when finally she spoke.

'Everything and nothing, Daniel. Everything, because you kept back maybe the biggest piece of you from me, and nothing, because I finally realise that you're never going to open up. You knew me, you knew about my family, my friends, my fears, and looking back I can see that I knew nothing about you—nothing at all. You're just not prepared to share.'

'Share?' He gave a scornful, mirthless laugh. 'God, Louise, things happen and we move on. We don't all have to go over and over things to reach some sort of resolution. It happened, I dealt with it and I moved on—it's that simple.' And there was no answer, because Daniel didn't even think there was a problem. Clearly he thought it really was that simple. 'It never entered my head that Declan was my son, because I thought I couldn't have children.'

'Well, you can.' There wasn't a trace of irony in her voice, just wretched, wretched pain, because even if they had once adored one another, clearly they hadn't known each other. Clearly he hadn't trusted her enough to tell her the truth. 'And you did.'

'You should have told me, Louise.' It was as if all the fight had left him, the anger gone, replaced now by the sheer overwhelming sadness and terror that Louise recognised because she was feeling it, too. Sadness for what he'd missed out on and terror for what he might now never have. 'And nothing, *nothing* you can say will ever change that. You *know* that you should have told me.'

She opened her mouth to argue, to explain again how impossible he had made it for her, but even before the words were formed she choked them back, knowing in her heart of hearts that he was right, knowing that no matter how difficult it might have been, she should never have denied him the chance to be Declan's father. That this proud, complicated man had deserved the chance to know.

'I'm sorry.' She whispered the two words, two barely audible words that were utterly heartfelt, but Daniel shook his head.

'I'll never forgive you for this, Louise.' His face was utterly stricken but his eyes were unwavering as they stared back at her. 'If I never get to hold my son, I swear I will never forgive you.'

Harsh words perhaps, but staring back at him all she could manage was a tiny nod. An acknowledgement that she understood because somehow, if the roles could be reversed, if somehow he could have denied her pregnancy, the gift of bringing a life into the world and those precious weeks of Declan's short life—she'd be saying those very words, too.

CHAPTER TEN

'A DIFFICULT procedure.'

'A lot of gangrenous bowel. Fortunately, at this stage, we didn't proceed to colostomy.'

'Still in Recovery.'

'Critical but stable.'

Words seemed to be coming at Louise like bullets, but she deflected each painful one and clung to the positive instead, just the fact he had made it through, that her tiny son had made it through something so massive and lay just a few metres away a miracle in itself.

'Can I see him?'

'Not yet.' Mr Masterson shook his head. 'He's only just been wheeled out of the operating theatre. There are a lot of staff around him and tubes—'

'I think Louise and I both know what a post-operative patient looks like,' Daniel cut in, somehow managing to be authoritative even as his whole world spun out of control. 'We won't get in the way.'

'Of course.'

It was definitely a professional courtesy to a fellow consultant surgeon, one that never in a million years would have been extended to a new bank nurse on the surgical ward, but Louise couldn't have cared less. As Daniel nodded to her and led the way through to the recovery area, all she knew was that she would be seeing her son again, her shaking legs almost running the short distance. But as they walked through the doors, as she glimpsed Declan's limp body on a paediatric warmer, for a second Louise decided that maybe Mr Masterson had been right—that no mother should ever have to see her child like this.

Hooked up to a ventilator, Declan was completely naked with not even a blanket to cover him, just overhead lights to bring up his body temperature. Monitors that were usually familiar only alarmed her now as she watched the green bleeps, the rapid tracing of his heartbeat, his breathing, his blood-pressure readings and oxygen saturations, relaying information that right now she was too confused to interpret. Instead, Louise forced herself to look at Declan, tried to fathom that this still little body had suckled from her breast just hours before, so warm and full of life in her arms.

And now look at him.

A large dressing covered the wound on his swollen abdomen with drain tubes coming out, a catheter to monitor his fragile fluid output and drips in each flaccid arm, Hartmann's solution in one and blood going through the other. And somewhere in the middle was her tiny little son.

And Daniel's, too.

Hospitals were not exactly renowned for keeping the lid on a good piece of gossip and clearly everyone had heard the rumours because the staff stepped back a touch as he stepped forward, his face absolutely unreadable as Daniel tentatively held out a hand and touched Declan's waxy cheek. With infinite tenderness, he lowered his dark head and whispered something for his baby's ears only.

'We really need to get on.' The theatre sister's words were kind but firm, her eyes on Louise, who stood frozen to the spot. 'If you want to give him a quick kiss now, that's fine, then you can see him again once he's in Intensive Care.'

Since Elaine had told her the news, all she had wanted had been to touch him, to feel him, but now that she could, now that the moment was there, Louise was more terrified than she'd ever been in her life. She could feel the impatient eyes of the staff on her, knew that if she didn't touch him now then she'd be denied it for hours, maybe for ever, and yet still she stood there, inexplicable perhaps to all but someone who had to see their baby so fragile and so very, very ill.

'Just touch his cheek, Louise.' Daniel's low voice jerked her out of inaction, his strong arm around her shoulder, gently propelling her forward, holding her up, taking her hand and guiding it to Declan's face. Then instinct took over, need overcame fear and she sank her face to his, felt the tiny dark curls tickling her cheeks, and somehow, despite the antiseptic, the scent of baby shampoo filled her nostrils. She recalled bathing him, her fingers working the lather in his little scalp. She inhaled that delicious baby smell and recognised her child all over again.

'I'm so, so, sorry.' She whispered it to him, not just because she hadn't known that his cries had been more sinister than she'd realised, not just because of all the pain he must surely be in, but because Louise knew that this little boy *had* deserved to know his father.

Had deserved to be loved by the most wonderful, difficult man in the world.

'Come on, Louise.' his arm was still around her, guiding her out of the recovery area and back to the ghastly blandness of the waiting room. As they reached the door he let her glimpse luxury—held her in his arms for a second so small it was barely there, let her glimpse the bliss of sharing the love of a child with another—took over the reins in the moment she needed it most. 'He'll be OK.' He said the words into her hair, strong, calm, solid words that for a slice of time reassured her. She leant on him, relished the moment that he carried the pain for both of them. Glimpsed what she'd missed through her pregnancy, through the long, lonely, painful hours of childbirth and the months that had followed—glimpsed being a mother with a partner by her side. But all too soon it was over and Daniel released her. She stepped back into the waiting room and sat on the seat, waiting for him to join her, but Daniel turned on his heel and walked away.

'Where are you going?'

He barely stopped, just turned his head, the shutters completely down now, the glimpse of closeness completely eradicated by the cool look he threw at her.

'That's not your concern, Louise.'

CHAPTER ELEVEN

'How is he?' Maggie asked a few days later, appearing round the door of the side ward of the children's ward with a bright smile, producing *decent* coffee and genuine warmth just when it was needed most.

'Good. He took a good feed,' an exhausted Louise replied, peeling open a brown paper bag and staring at the contents as if they were rancid.

'Chicken and avocado foccacia,' Maggie said. 'Your favourite.'

'I'm not hungry.'

'You've hardly eaten for days.' There was a slight edge to Maggie's voice. At the beginning and end of each of her shifts since Declan had been hospitalised Maggie had been appearing with various delicacies from the café opposite the hospital, but even the mere smell of food was enough to make Louise gag, and with a tired shake of her head she put down the bag and gave a sigh. 'Maybe I'll warm it up later.'

'Maybe,' Maggie said tightly. 'Or more than likely the second I'm gone you're going to throw it in the bin.'

'I'm just not hungry.'

Thankfully Maggie didn't pursue it, just sat down on one

of the plastic seats and gazed at the little guy who'd had everyone so worried. 'Kids are amazing, aren't they? They bounce back so quickly. Looking at him, it's hard to believe just how sick he was.'

'He still is.' It was Louise who had an edge to her voice now. With each drip or tube that came down, with each gigantic step of progress Declan made, the more nervous she became, knowing that in a couple of days it would be time to leave the hospital, time to 'get back to normal', and it did nothing but daunt her. He'd spent two hellish days clinging to life in Intensive Care, his tiny body battling to cope with the massive assault that had been placed on it. But slowly he had responded and it was as if Louise's own body had shut down—her breast milk almost drying up, her tears long since over, her emotions for everyone bar Declan put on hold. She just stared dry-eyed into the cot and willed him to respond, to pull through as an endless stream of people paraded in and out—nurses, doctors, physios, her family driving down from the country, Maggie, social workers and, of course, Daniel. With eyes only for his son, he avoided talking to her, any questions about Declan's progress saved for the staff. But apart from his remoteness towards her, what worried her most was the proprietorial way he dealt with Declan. Picking him up uninvited when he started to wake, changing his nappy, even taking a bottle of expressed breast milk and feeding him one time when Louise had darted to the loo.

Letting it be known without words that he was very much in this little boy's life.

As if on cue, Maggie asked about him.

'Has Daniel been in today?'

'Yep.' Louise ran a tired hand through her rather greasy hair. 'He spent an hour with him—he had the bloody nerve to ask me to leave the room, said that he wanted some time with his son alone.'

'And did you?'

'I didn't have much choice—he can be pretty direct.'

'He *is* his father,' Maggie pointed out. 'Has he spoken to you at all?'

'No.' Louise shook her head. 'Apart from "Pass me a baby wipe" he hasn't really said a word. You know, I don't know how I ended up the bad guy here. He was the one who dumped me, remember—he was the one who said that the last thing on his agenda was settling down and having children…'

'You know why now,' Maggie said patiently. 'Louise, even if you two were only together a short while, you were both incredibly close. It must hurt like hell to know that you chose not to tell him.'

'He *chose* not to tell me about his cancer,' Louise retorted. 'He *chose* not to tell me things, too.'

'Well, maybe he had his reasons,' Maggie said. 'And it's good that he's here to give you a break every now and then.'

'Did you call the real estate agent?' Louise asked, firmly changing the subject.

'The house has gone, Louise. The new tenants have already moved in. Don't worry about that for now—you know you can come back to the flat.'

'Have you found someone?'

'No.' Maggie smiled, and even though Louise knew she was lying, she was too exhausted to care.

At least they had a home to go to.

'What you need is to go home for a few hours and have a nice long bath and then go to bed.'

'I'm not leaving him,' Louise insisted, knowing what

was coming next because Maggie had been pushing the point for a couple of days now, insisting that she go home for a few hours.

'So you're just going to sit here getting thinner and smellier?'

'There are showers here!' Louise pointed out.

'Ah, but no razors—'

'I've got more important things to do than shave my legs' Louise snapped.

'Look.' Maggie was completely unfazed by her snappish response. 'Declan's long since out of Intensive Care and everyone says that he's doing marvellously. Why don't you go home for a few hours—have a nice shower and a change of clothes and grab some sleep. I'll stay with him, I promise, and if anything happens—'

'I don't want to leave him,' Louise said again.

'Well, I happen to think that's a very good idea.'

A deep voice filled the room—and that distinctive after-shave—and Louise jerked her eyes to where Daniel stood, his immaculate and polished appearance only exacerbating how truly awful she must surely look. 'In fact, I think you should go home for the night and have a proper rest.'

'No!' Immediately she shook her head. 'Absolutely not.'

'I'll stay with him,' Daniel said, equally firmly.

'I've never spent a night away from him,' Louise argued, 'and I'm certainly not about to start when he's in hospital!'

Utterly unmoved by her statement, he turned to Maggie, who was fiddling with a cup of water and trying to pretend she wasn't listening. 'Maggie, could I have a word with Louise alone, please?'

No!

She didn't want to be alone with him, didn't want to hear whatever it was that he had to say, because she knew, just knew that she wasn't going to like it. But even faithful Maggie was deserting her. With a tiny shrug her friend picked up her bag *and* the coffee and the chicken and avocado foccacia, and headed to the corridor outside, clearly expecting Daniel to talk her around, clearly expecting Louise to join her in a couple of moments.

Well, no way.

'Here.' Unlike hers, Daniel's hand was completely steady and with a frown deepening on her face Louise took the cheque he was holding out to her and stared at the ludicrously large sum.

'What's this?'

'Child support,' Daniel clipped. 'I've spoken to my lawyer and it's been back paid from the day he was born.'

'Your lawyer?' She gasped the words out, scarcely able to believe it had come to this, that he'd really thought it was necessary. 'What the hell did you go and see a lawyer for?'

'Do I really need to tell you that?'

'Daniel, I'm not going to stop you from seeing him—I'd never do that!'

'But you did.' Utterly unmoved, he stared back at her. 'And I'm not prepared to take any chances, Louise. I'm seeing my lawyer to hopefully sort this mess out and in the meantime I'll pay—'

'I don't want it.' She tried to push the cheque back at him, but Daniel just stood still, his hand loose by his sides. 'And I don't want to leave him tonight—'

'Let's get one thing clear, Louise.' Those gorgeous blue eyes that had once adored her were cold and direct as they stared back at her, that gorgeous body that had, just a few nights ago, been pressed against hers now stood remote and tense just a few feet away. And the abyss between them widened ever further as his clipped, measured tones spelt things out. 'This isn't about what you want and it isn't about what I want—it's about Declan. And whether you like it or not, Louise, he has a father, a father who *will* support him and spend time with him. You can't work at the moment, so you clearly need some money, so why not spare us both the point-less arguments and cash the cheque?'

God, she wished she was in a position to refuse, but Daniel was right—she did need the money. As full as her head had been with Declan's health, as he had started to improve, the practicalities of being a casual worker with no income had started to impinge. Sick baby or no sick baby, the rent still had to be paid, nappies needed to be bought. The world didn't stop turning just because Louise's had.

'Thank you.' With an attempt at dignity she placed the cheque in her bag. 'But—'

'No buts.' Still he stood resolute. 'I'm staying with him to-night.'

Again she wished she was in a position to argue, but it was as if all the emotion she had struggled to keep in check over the past few days bubbled to the fore. Tears that had been swal-lowed down were brimming in her bloodshot, exhausted eyes, the adrenaline that had fizzed through her veins, that had kept her going, was turning off as easily as a tap. Overwhelming fatigue set in in an instant and, whether she liked it or not, Louise knew that he was right, knew that if she was going to be any good for Declan tomorrow, tonight she needed her bed. But, most surprisingly of all for Louise, she knew that if it had been anyone apart from Daniel, she'd have refused. Her mother, her sisters and Maggie had offered endlessly to stay with Declan, practically begging her to go home for a few hours, and she'd always refused. Yet here she was saying good-night to her son and knowing she wouldn't see him till the morning. It could mean only one thing—she trusted Daniel.

Completely.

And as she watched Daniel walk over and sit beside the cot, watched as he stretched his tired body out in the chair beside his son's cot then pulled down the side and closed his big strong hand around Declan's tiny one, Louise knew something else.

That despite the distance he had from the start placed between them, still she loved him—always had and always would.

Maybe he felt her eyes on him because he looked over and she braced herself for a few sharp words, but they never came. Instead, he gave her a tiny ghost of a smile, eyes that had been so cold now bordering on compassionate as she stood there. 'He'll be OK, Louise, and you know if there's a problem, I'll call you.'

'I know.' Her voice was small.

'You really do need to get some rest.'

'I know that, too.' Louise nodded, tears swimming in her eyes as she stared at the two men she loved most in the world, hovering on the outskirts of their closeness as if staring through the window of an intimate party she hadn't been invited to. She'd never felt so useless in her life, so utterly and completely replaceable. She turned to go, but just as she did so he called her back.

'What do I need to know?' As she frowned, he elaborated. 'What are you going to remember in a couple of hours and panic because you didn't tell me?'

He knew her so well.

'My milk's in the fridge—the nurses will warm it up. And he likes his blanket right up around his shoulders,' Louise said hesitantly, grateful, so grateful that he wasn't taking over completely, was acknowledging that she knew Declan best. 'And sometimes when he starts to wake up it's not because he's hungry, just that he can't find his thumb. If you pop it back in his mouth for him, he sometimes settles back to sleep, and he likes to have his forehead stroked…'

'I'd worked that one out already,' Daniel said, but without a trace of malice. 'You have a good rest and don't race to get back here in the morning—I've arranged some cover.'

He turned back to Declan then, two dark heads close together, two people who belonged to each other no matter how much she'd tried to convince herself that they didn't.

'I am sorry, Daniel.' He stiffened but didn't turn. 'I know now how wrong I was not to tell you…'

'Let's just leave it for now.' Still he didn't look at her. 'Let's just get through the next few weeks, shall we, and concentrate on getting Declan well.'

Again, it wasn't as if she had much choice.

CHAPTER TWELVE

'I'LL just have a quick shower,' Louise protested as Maggie guided her to the bathroom.

'You'll do no such thing,' Maggie chided, opening the door on a scented, steam-filled room and a bath that was barely visible, overflowing with bubbles. 'You're going to soak till the water goes warm and you're going shave your legs and wash your hair and not come out till you're all shiny and wrinkled, and *then* you're going to eat something.'

'I just want to sleep,' Louise protested but, as gentle and as kind as Maggie could be, right now she was wearing her strict *I will not be argued with* psychiatric nurse's face. With a rather feeble sigh Louise nodded, closing the door on her and peeling off her clothes, before sinking into the way-too-hot water and finding it was actually rather nice after all.

'Better?' Maggie asked *much* later when a yawning Louise appeared, wrapped in her bathrobe and rubbing her hair with a towel.

'Much! And you were right.' Louise even managed a smile. 'I did need to shave my legs!'

'Now you can eat,' Maggie instructed, and heaven knows what had happened to her because, instead of a pizza box or shiny take-away cartons, there was a huge bowl of creamy mushroom soup and a mountain of crusty bread, and as Louise started to eat, she found out that she actually was hungry after all. Starving even!

'Have a glass of wine!' Maggie offered, pushing a glass to her, but just as she was about to shake her head Maggie shook hers. 'You're not feeding him tonight.'

'Don't remind me,' Louise groaned. 'I'm actually really struggling to feed him—he's being given too many bottles.'

'Then give it up!'

'I don't want to—I'd miss it.'

'What, miss leaking boobs and feeling like a walking cow?'

'You have such a nice way of putting things,' Louise answered tartly.

'When do you think you'll be back at work?'

'A couple of weeks.' Louise shrugged. 'Certainly not before.'

'If you need a loan to help with the rent or anything…' Maggie offered, and Louise felt a stupid great lump in her throat. Maggie was perpetually broke, juggling credit cards with frightening skill and constantly hanging out for payday, and yet here she was offering Louise a share of what she didn't have.

'I'm OK for money,' Louise said, but Maggie wasn't having it.

'Don't go all proud on me,' Maggie admonished. 'I know things are going to be tight with you not working, but we *will* manage. I can—'

'Maggie, look!' Just to stop her worrying, Louise leant into her bag and pulled out the cheque Daniel had given her, chewing nervously on her bottom lip as Maggie's eyes widened at the sum. 'It's child support backdated since

Declan's birth. I didn't want to accept it but, as Daniel pointed out, I don't exactly have much choice.'

'You are entitled to it,' Maggie said, and for the first time since Declan's operation she said the wrong thing, hit a nerve that was so painfully raw Louise visibly winced, great salty tears welling up and spilling out onto her cheeks, followed by a strangled sob as Maggie, who was usually totally unfazed by emotional outbursts, sat reeling at the pain evident in her friend's tears, her face visibly shocked as Louise cried as if she'd never stop.

'You're going to blur the ink.' Maggie attempted a joke, took the cheque from Louise's clenched hands and wrapped her arms around her friend. 'Louise, what on earth is wrong? And, please, don't tell me it's nothing.'

'Isn't having a sick child and his father hating me enough to be going on with?'

'Daniel doesn't hate you,' Maggie insisted. 'He's just hurt and confused, but in time he'll come around. Even if you two aren't going to be together, I just know you're going to make wonderful parents.'

'He lives in England.' Louise gulped. 'He's only supposed to be here for a year.'

'He'll probably relocate.' But as Louise's face crumpled Maggie got firm, held her by the shoulders and demanded to know what was going on. 'Louise, just what the hell are you so scared of?'

'Ruining his life,' Louise muttered, words bubbling up in her throat. Taking a deep breath, finally she let them out and told Maggie what she'd been holding in since her pregnancy test had showed a little pink cross. 'The same way my dad's lover ruined his.'

Thankfully Maggie didn't push things, must have realised the mammoth effort it had taken to unburden just this much. Instead, she guided Louise to the bedroom and drew the curtains as her exhausted friend fell into bed. Then she disappeared, only to re-emerge a couple of minutes later with a glass of water and a box of tissues.

'I've rung the ward and spoken to Daniel. Declan's just had his antibiotics and last feed and has fallen sound asleep. He says that you're not to worry or rush in tomorrow, just sleep till you wake up.'

'Did he say anything else?' Louise checked. 'You didn't tell him anything I said?'

'Louise, I was on the phone for thirty seconds, if that—hardly time for an in-depth discussion. And really you didn't tell me anything I hadn't already worked out for myself. Now there's nothing for you to do now except go to sleep. Daniel's taking care of Declan tonight—there's nothing for you to worry about.'

There wasn't, Louise realised as the door softly closed, and for the first time in ages there wasn't the hiss and whir of an IV drip or the snuffly breathing of Declan to keep her awake, no nurses bustling in with torches blazing or phones going off at the end of the ward. Oh, sure, if she'd had the energy, there were no doubt a million and one things she could have concerned herself with, but tonight it was bliss just to close her eyes on everything and drift off to sleep, knowing that Declan was safe with Daniel.

That for now all was well.

'Wow!' Daniel's smile as Louise burst into the ward at eleven the next morning stopped her in her tracks. 'Look at you—you look like a new woman!'

Having woken at ten, she'd yelped in alarm at she'd eyed the clock, utterly appalled that she'd slept for so long, only to find Maggie, completely oblivious to her horror, calmly buttering toast and offering her a cup of tea, telling her that Daniel had said to take her time.

He may have said that to Maggie, Louise had thought as she'd been dropped off at the hospital entrance and raced along the polished corridors, but no doubt he had a social worker sitting there at the cot side with her stopwatch in hand, about to inform her what a terrible mother she was for even *thinking* of sleeping while her baby lay ill in hospital.

'I'm sorry I'm so late,' Louise panted, curiously deflated that Declan wasn't screaming in protest at her prolonged absence. Instead, he lay giggling and cooing up at Daniel who was, with surprising ease, changing his nappy. 'I think Maggie swiped my alarm clock and then she insisted I have some breakfast before she drove me—'

'Louise!' Daniel halted her flood of excuses. 'It's fine. I did say take your time.' Picking up Declan, he handed him to her. Her whole body fizzed with love as she took his pudgy, scented body and held it, feeling his little fingers twining into her dark curls, seeing the rapt adoration in his face as he welcomed her back.

'You've lost weight, Louise.'

'Oh!' It wasn't Daniel's comment that floored her—she already knew she'd lost weight because everything had hung off her when she'd got dressed that morning and she was now wearing jeans she'd only aspired to, only to find out that even they were too big. No, it was the fact that he'd noticed, the rather personal observation that had her blushing to the roots of her now newly washed hair as she felt his eyes drift over her body.

'I'm thinking of writing to one of the women's magazines,' Louise answered, still breathless but for entirely different reasons as Daniel frowned with bemusement at her comment. 'Well, I've tried every other post-pregnancy diet and none of them worked, but this one's been just a breeze—the weight's just fallen off!' They shared a tiny glimmer of a smile—her slightly offbeat humour still able to bring that out in him at least. 'What happened on the ward round?

'His stitches can come out tomorrow and if things carry on progressing well, the day after tomorrow he can go home.'

'It's too soon,' Louise gasped, terrified yet pleased all the same that he was doing so well, and so quickly, too.

'He's tough.' Daniel smiled warmly, only it was aimed at his son.

'Anything else happen while I was away?'

'Your parents came.'

'Together?' Louise gasped. 'They both came to see me together?' She'd known her mother was coming but she could scarcely believe that they'd both been here. But her brief flare of hope was doused before it even formed as Daniel shook his head.

'Er, yes and no. Your mum came first, followed a few moments later by your father…'

'How long did they stay?'

'About a minute. Your mum's coming back at lunchtime and I think your father said he'd try to be back later this afternoon.'

'I'm sorry if they made you uncomfortable. Believe me, it had nothing to do with you being here. I don't think they've been in the same room together for the last decade.'

'Do they know?' Daniel asked. 'About me, I mean.'

'I told Mum after Declan's operation.' She was scuffing the

floor with her foot, glad to smother her face in Declan's warm body as she faced this most difficult conversation.

'And what did she say?'

Louise's face was practically purple, and even if he couldn't see her, she was positive he could feel the heat from the blush that was scorching through her body.

'Daniel, you don't want to know.'

'Screw him for every cent?' He was so spot on she could only wince and close her eyes, missing his small smile.

'Something like that,' Louise mumbled.

'Well, I'd better go and earn a living, then! I'm joking, Louise,' he added as she cringed a touch more. 'I know it was just your mother talking. Right, I've cancelled all my theatre lists till the end of this week so I can stay again tonight.'

'There's really no need,' Louise said. 'I feel fine now I've had a good sleep.'

'I want to stay,' Daniel said, giving Declan a little tickle as he spoke. 'And given that he's going to be home in the next couple of days, I think you should try and cram in as much sleep as you can. You're going to be run ragged the next couple of weeks with a restless baby, outpatient appointments…'

'Finding a solicitor,' Louise added, taking a deep breath and forcing herself to look at him.

'Is it really necessary, Louise? Can't we just sort this out between us?'

'You've seen one,' Louise pointed out.

'I had to. I want to support him properly and I doubt you'd have taken the cheque otherwise…'

'Probably' she admitted. 'Look, maybe we could leave it for a few weeks—just concentrate on getting him well and you can drop in to see him whenever you want.'

His lips brushed the top of Declan's head, dusting his curls with the softest, most tender of kisses to say goodbye, and as his face moved, Louise again realised all she was missing out on.

'There is one other thing—about me "dropping in".' His hand hovered on the door he had opened and briefly he turned around. 'When he's discharged, you're both coming to stay at my house.'

'Excuse me?' If it hadn't been Declan she was holding, she'd surely have dropped him. 'You don't have any say as to where I live!'

'But I have a huge say as to where my son lives!' A picture of rational composure, he stared back, completely unmoved by her angry protest. 'Louise, we've both agreed to concentrate on getting Declan well for the next few weeks—now, given he's recovering from a life-threatening incident, surely you can see that a third-floor flat with an out-of-order lift isn't suitable accommodation.'

'Daniel, we *cannot* live together,' Louise argued, but it fell on deaf ears.

'Louise, I can assure you there won't be any cosy nights sitting on the sofa and trying to make things work out for us— you don't have to even talk to me if you don't want to. This isn't about you and I—it's about Declan, and giving him the best possible chance for a smooth recovery. I won't take no for an answer, Louise. You'll be coming home with me.'

CHAPTER THIRTEEN

THOUGH, never in a million years, would Louise admit it to Daniel, it was actually a relief to be living at his house. For the first time since the pregnancy test had been positive—actually, for the first time since Daniel had cruelly ended things—she had the tiniest glimpse of a peaceful existence.

There was no stress about suitable accommodation—Daniel's executive residence had *all* the creature comforts. There was money in her bank account and Declan's future was looking pretty secure—but more than that, so much more than that, despite the tension between them, despite the long, strained silences and the palpable animosity, it was as if a huge burden had been lifted.

Daniel loved Declan.

The overwhelming responsibility of parenthood was just so much easier shared. There was someone to assess and then calm her when Declan threw up the second night he was home, someone to share her excitement when a sliver of a tooth appeared in his bottom gum, and the knowledge that if something terrible happened to her, Declan would always be loved.

OK, it couldn't last much longer—living with Daniel and barely talking not really a viable option—but it *had* been nice to concentrate on Declan's recovery in a state of relative peace. Although Maggie had been completely and utterly brilliant—the best friend a girl could have—it was absolute bliss to turn off the shower at seven a.m. and not have to race to hush Declan when he started yelling!

Daniel would pick him up!

Combing her damp hair and *luxuriously* brushing her teeth, Louise briefly contemplated getting dressed, but Declan's screams were getting louder as Daniel's attempts to soothe worked less and less.

'Someone wants you badly!' Daniel gave a relieved eye roll as, wrapped in a towel, she padded into the living room, trying and failing not to notice just how fabulous he looked. Dressed in nothing but a pair of boxers, he was standing in the middle of the room unshaven and unkempt, still blinking from sleep as Declan cried even louder. 'He's starving!'

'No wonder,' Louise said, taking one very angry man from one very exhausted one. 'He slept through the night for the first time!' Aware she was dressed only in a very skimpy towel, Louise intended to dart to the bedroom for a feed. But Declan had other ideas, his head butting at her chest, fat hands grabbing at the towel, and it was just *easier* to plonk herself on the sofa and feed him—silence mercifully filling the room in a second or two.

'He slept all night?'

'Yep.' Louise wasn't looking up, just concentrating on Declan. 'And so did I—it was wonderful!'

'Do you want coffee?'

'Please.' Louise nodded, her mind not really on Daniel but sort of peripherally aware, expecting Daniel to move, expecting him to head off to the kitchen, to hear the kettle flick on and *hopefully* the click of the toaster if she was lucky. But after a second or two when he still hadn't moved, she was suddenly *very* aware, her dark brown eyes looking up and catching his.

'What?'

'I just…' Daniel gave a shrug. 'Are you worried about starting work tomorrow?'

'To be honest, I haven't even thought about it. Normally I'd be tying my hair in knots at the thought of starting in a different department, but the only thing I'm stressing about is leaving Declan in the crèche. Mind you, I'm sure, given what's happened, they'll call me if they're at all concerned.'

'Or me,' Daniel said. 'I've given the crèche my pager number.'

'OK…' Well, of course he would have!

'What are you doing today?'

Louise frowned at his further question. Normally they spoke only talked about Declan.

'I'm looking at houses again.'

'Oh, right.'

'I think I've found one, too.'

'Close?'

'Yep.' Louise nodded. 'And very suitable.'

'And then?' He registered her frown. 'Only I finish at two today. My theatre list had been cancelled so I thought maybe we could go…' he gave an uneasy shrug '…to the park or something.'

'Sorry, I've got an appointment.' Louise shook her head, taking great interest in feeding Declan again as she lied through her teeth. 'With my gynaecologist.'

'But you saw him last week.'

'I've seen him most weeks since I had Declan,' Louise gulped, watching as even her left boob blushed at her fib.

'Sorry.' Daniel winced. 'I didn't mean to pry. I'll come home and look after Declan for you.'

'You don't have to.'

'I want to.'

Why did he have to be so nice when she was lying? Louise asked herself guiltily

'Everything's fine, isn't it, Louise? I mean, if there are any, er, *problems*, I can refer you to someone. You really ought to see—'

'I can find my own gynaecologist,' Louise bristled. 'Are you going to make that coffee?'

'You make sure you go!' Ruth Andrews's impatience was thinly disguised as her voice shrilled down the telephone line from country Victoria to Melbourne almost the second after Daniel had left for work.

'Mum, I really think I might make things worse. He knows I'm looking at houses this morning. He hasn't even hinted that he wants custody.'

'What if he doesn't pay you maintenance next week? What if he just decides to stop?'

'He wouldn't,' Louise insisted, 'and, anyway, I managed before, I'd manage again—I start back at work tomorrow.'

'That's not the point!'

'Mum, I would have thought, given the pressure Dad's maintenance payments placed on your marriage, you'd understand.' Ah, but bitterness had no logic. Louise had already long since worked that one out, and her mother had nearly thirty years' worth all stored up for this very moment.

'You need to get some legal advice! What if he decides he's the better parent? What if he decides his home's more suitable than the one you find?' Ruth pushed on, and Louise closed her eyes in horror as her mother articulated her darkest fears.

'What if he decides that England might be a nicer place to raise his son?'

'OK, I'll go!' Louise broke in, seeing the blurry logic her mother was offering and reluctantly admitting that she might be right. Even though she'd told Daniel she'd wait a while before contacting anyone, as her mother and every other friend/armchair attorney who had gladly foisted an opinion on her had warned, she was crazy to wait for him to make a move. For Declan's sake, she had to know where she stood!

Exhausted from a morning of house-hunting, Louise wearily surveyed her wardrobe. A suit seemed a bit over the top, but she didn't want go the other way and arrive on the solicitor's doorstep in jeans and a T-shirt, looking like a refugee, so she decided to attempt her 'posh frock'. Well, not posh exactly—a simply navy linen shift dress that was dragged out for interviews and funerals. As Louise slipped her old faithful on, she was delighted to see that it fitted her perfectly. OK, maybe a touch too short, but it was simple yet elegant, and made the very best of her newly found waistline. After pulling her hair into a simple chignon, for the first time since Declan's illness Louise opened her make-up bag. She applied a light foundation, deciding she looked like a ghost and that she might need iron tablets, but, for now touch of blusher would have to suffice. A lick of mascara and a slick of lip gloss and Louise surveyed herself in the mirror, deciding that she actually quite liked what she saw—not exactly a 'yummy mummy', as Maggie always hopefully suggested, but she'd do for now. As Daniel came through the front door, clearly he thought the same.

'You look nice,' he commented, as she filled up her handbag with keys, purse and lipstick, and put in her earrings at the same time.

'Thanks,' Louise mumbled, hoping he wouldn't offer her a lift and wondering what on earth she'd say if he did. But after his brief greeting Daniel had eyes only for Declan, heading straight over to the baby mat on the floor where the little boy lay, kicking his little legs in the air and squealing with delight as Daniel grabbed his feet and started tickling them. 'He's just been fed,' Louise warned, envisaging regurgitated milk on Daniel's smart navy suit. 'Oh, and there's a bottle in the fridge if you need it.'

'He'll be fine.' Daniel waved her away. 'You go and do whatever you have to. Enjoy yourself.'

'Hardly!'

He *actually* smiled.

After the longest air-conditioned wait, filling in forms, then thumbing glossy and unusually up-to-date magazines and crossing her ankles nervously, she was shown through to a spacious office. And when she'd been offered a glass of iced water that had arrived in crystal, Louise started to sweat at the thought of the sizeable bill that would surely arrive in a few days' time.

Greeted by an immaculate woman who clearly believed in power dressing, Louise was infinitely grateful that she hadn't opted for jeans!

'You were lucky to get in to see me so soon!' The solicitor flashed very white porcelain caps across the table. 'I was booked for court this afternoon but it's been adjourned. Now, how can I help you?'

Barely looking up, she took copious notes as Louise explained the reason for her visit, but Louise noted with distaste that she did look up and give a glint of a smile when Louise divulged Daniel's job title.

'The baby's father's a *consultant* surgeon?'

'That's right.' Louise gulped, her stomach sinking as Ms Corporate Suit buzzed on her intercom and asked for more coffee and biscuits to be brought in—*cream* biscuits.

She should have felt reassured by the time she stepped out of the office and into the sultry late afternoon heat. Should have been relieved to find out that she had nothing really to worry about. Access visits would be arranged and Declan's financial future was secure, and in a couple of days a nice thick letter would be landing on Daniel's solicitor's desk, out-lining what Louise considered *reasonable* and awaiting his response, but instead all she felt was sick.

Sick to her stomach.

In a couple of days the games would begin and it would truly be all over for them bar the shouting—the lease was already signed on her new home, a letter was being typed by her solicitor's secretary—the whole world was pulling them apart when all she wanted was for them to be together.

But could she tell him?

'Yummy mummy!' Maggie grinned as Louise walked into Daniel's living room. Her elegant chignon had long since unfurled in the humid heat and, no doubt, her make-up was sliding down her face. Although normally Louise would have been delighted to see Maggie, she was hard pushed to feign a smile when all she wanted to do was talk to Daniel.

'What are you doing here?'

'I got stood up! So I thought I'd come around for tea and sympathy but you weren't home—so I got a cold beer and a male perspective instead!' She raised her drink to Daniel and winked. 'Where have you been?'

'To the gynae.'

'Again!' Maggie gave a little shudder. 'Hence the dress!'

'Did Glynn ring and cancel?' Louise asked, trying quickly to change the subject, giving a brief smile at Daniel and frowning when all she got was a very cool look back.

'No!' Maggie didn't even attempt to gloss over it, just rolled her eyes at Daniel who was sipping on a beer as well, his face dark and moody, absolutely refusing to look at Louise now. 'Bastard!' Maggie continued, utterly oblivious of the tension.

'Maybe he got caught up at work,' Louise offered. 'Or maybe he forgot which night it was supposed to be.'

'Maybe I should stop making excuses for his bad behaviour,' Maggie said stoutly, nodding to Daniel, who gave a grim smile back. 'He's always late—if he shows up at all, that is. He takes for ever to buy a round of drinks and—' As if on cue, her mobile phone rang and Maggie answered it, her eyebrows in her hairline as she listened to whoever it was on the other end. 'No, thanks,' she said finally. 'No, thanks,' she said again, and with a rather pained sigh went in for the kill. 'I'm not making myself very clear, am I? When hell freezes over!' And clicking off the phone, she stood up and laughed at Louise's shocked expression. 'Right, I'd better be off.'

'You're welcome to stay,' Louise started, then snapped her mouth closed. It wasn't exactly her place to ask and, anyway, she really needed to speak to Daniel. Maggie shook her head.

'I'm off to a singles' bar tonight!'

'He might have just been caught up, Maggie,' Louise said. 'Give the guy a chance.'

'He's had his chance,' Maggie said, picking up her bag and calling over her shoulder. 'I'm holding out for Mr Perfect.'

'There's no such thing,' Louise called back good-humouredly, but Maggie as always had the last word.

'Say that again when we're fifty, honey, and I'm lying by the pool with some bronzed god massaging body oil into my liposuctioned body…'

'That he paid for!' They said it in unison—the same conversation replayed each time one of Maggie's romances ended.

Normally it made Daniel laugh—she'd expected a thin smile at least—but when Louise glanced over he was still sulking in his corner with a big black stormcloud gathering over his head. They'd lived in practical silence for two weeks now. Long, long gaps in conversation, more than a few hundred uncomfortable moments, but when the tornado that was Maggie had left the building Louise knew that this time it was different, the tension in the room so palpable Louise felt as if it was choking her. Daniel quietly watched her every move as she sat down and crossed and re-crossed her legs.

'How was Declan?' Louise asked, trying to break the silence, trying to lift the mood before she broached what was really on her mind.

'Fine.' Daniel gave a tight shrug. 'He's just gone down.'

Which took care of that!

'Something smells nice!' It did. A delicious herby aroma filled the tense air and for the first time Louise noticed the beautifully laid table, a bottle of wine chilling in the bucket, a beautiful arrangement of Australian native flowers filling a bowl in the centre, everything in place for a romantic evening—everything except the ambience.

'Daniel!' The note in her voice caught them both by surprise and Louise tried to reel it in, to defuse the urgency he must surely have heard. 'I was hoping,' Louise gave what she hoped was a casual shrug, 'that perhaps we could talk, after dinner maybe—it's nothing urgent.'

But it was urgent, a voice in her head reasoned.

Maggie was right to hold out for Mr Perfect—and yet she, Louise, had him right here in the living room, had their child sleeping a bedroom just a couple of metres away. But in a couple of days moments like this would be gone for ever, heated letters, followed by more heated letters and a day in court the only thing to look forward to.

No matter how difficult the mood, she *had* to talk to him.

'How was your doctor's appointment?' Daniel asked, very slowly, very deliberately.

'Long.' Louise blushed.

'And are there any problems I should know about? Anything you just didn't think to tell me?'

He knew, Louise realised. Somehow he knew where she'd been.

'Daniel…' She tried to push out the breath she was holding but it was trapped in her lungs. She tried to think of something to say to douse the rage that was simmering within him, but Daniel got there first.

'Did you tell her I was babysitting for you, Louise? That while you were at the *gynaecologist*, the bastard who did this to you was at home, looking after him?'

'I didn't mean to lie to you, Daniel.'

'I'm sure you didn't.' He shook his head, his mouth twisting in contempt as he stared at her. 'But you did it anyway. Again!'

Yes, she'd lied, yes, technically she was in the wrong, but this time when Daniel stood up and stormed towards his front door, Louise was right behind him. 'Walk away, why don't you?' Louise shouted. 'Again!'

Incredulous, he turned to face her, clearly shocked by her anger, clearly thinking he was in the right, but this time he wasn't, Louise decided. This time he'd damn well hear what she had to say.

'All I've ever done is love you.' She attempted a shout but it came out as a rasp. 'But every time I get close, you push me away. Every time I come close to measuring up, you set the bar higher.' Her voice was returning now, her finger jabbing him with each and every accusation. 'You dumped me, Daniel, and then you came here just a few weeks ago, made love to me, then walked out. You were the one who went to see a solicitor and now you are angry at me for doing the same!'

'You said you'd wait!' Daniel roared. 'Of course I saw a solicitor. You *forgot* to tell me you were having my baby.'

'Oh, I didn't forget.' Louise shook her head. 'I *decided* not to tell you.' Her fury was as great as his, David and Goliath perhaps, but in anger she matched him. 'I *chose* not to tell you because without warning or explanation you dumped me, Daniel. And, yes, I might have screwed up today, yes, I might have lied a little, but I have every right not to trust you after the way you treated me—every right!' White-lipped, she divided up all the guilt she'd taken for so long and placed his share firmly where it belonged. 'You took all the love we had and threw it away, leaving me to pick up the pieces. Well, one of the pieces was six pounds three ounces and, like it or not, I have to sort out his future.'

'Let's do it, then,' Daniel shouted, his face livid. 'Right here, right now, let's sort out his future. Marry me!'

It was absolutely the last thing she'd been expecting him to say and the complete antithesis of how a proposal should be, and she treated it with the contempt it deserved.

'Us—married!' She gave an incredulous, stunned, mirthless laugh. 'Daniel, we can't even go a couple of hours of being civil, so how the hell do you think we could make a marriage work?'

'Because he's our son, Louise,' Daniel spat out. 'Because he deserves to have two parents.'

'Whether or not we're married, Declan has two parents, Daniel,' she countered. The anger in him faded then his eyes implored her to listen to what he had to say, but every word just lacerated her more.

'Surely it's worth giving it a go for his sake? I don't want to lose him, Louise.'

'So you scream a proposal of marriage at me?' Wide-eyed, she stared at him as he balled his fists against his temples.

'It wasn't supposed to be like that.' He gestured to the table, to the flowers and wine, then pulled a box out of his hip pocket and opened it. Sapphires and diamonds twinkled at Louise through her tears. 'I was going to ask you properly and then your mother called—she left a message on the machine to see how you went at the solicitor's.'

It would have been so easy to blame her mother for the mess—too easy, perhaps—but the problems they'd created were entirely theirs.

'I walked back from the solicitor's feeling sick, Daniel.' Tears were coursing down her cheeks. 'Feeling sick because I didn't want it to end, feeling sick because I know you love Declan and, idiot that I am, I love you. I didn't want to end it, and if Maggie hadn't been here, you'd have known where I'd been straight away.'

'I want to believe you…'

'But you can't,' Louise said for him. 'And that's the whole bloody problem. Can you answer me a question?'

'Sure,' he offered easily, but his eyes didn't quite meet hers.

'What type of cancer did you have?'

Which was perhaps the strangest answer to a proposal ever, but for Louise it was simple—his answer was the litmus test that would give her her answer, because if he couldn't even reveal that, they hadn't a hope in hell.

'What on earth has that got to do with anything?' Daniel answered, shattering some of the last pieces of hope that held her heart together. 'Louise, just because I don't want to go over things, it doesn't mean I'm hiding anything. Maybe what you see really is what you get—and maybe, just maybe we could make this work.'

'Do you love me, Daniel?' Cutting directly to the chase, she stared right at him, every nerve taut, because never had she asked such a direct question and never had an answer mattered more.

'I care about you,' Daniel answered carefully, lacerating her with omission, smashing those last little pieces and crushing them completely. 'And when we were together I adored you. Can't that be enough to build on?' He took the ring out of its little nest and held it up to her, and there was a stricken dignity to her face as she slowly shook her head.

'Not for me.' She stared back at eyes that had adored but never really loved her, eyes that had always held back that little piece of him that she really needed. As hellish as it felt right now, Louise knew that she was making the right choice. That even if it meant lying by the pool alone and putting on her own suntan oil, true love was better than the half-life he was offering—hell, she'd pay for the liposuction herself.

'Please, Louise, just try it on.'

'No—because I don't particularly like sapphires.' She stared at the beastly ring and again shook her head. 'I'm sure it cost a fortune, I'm sure it will fit perfectly and that maybe in time I'd grow to be happy with it. I just never envisioned sapphires in my engagement ring.'

And he knew she wasn't talking about the ring, and she knew he was talking about himself when he offered to change it, but again she shook her head, stopped talking about the ring and told him exactly how she felt.

'No, because no matter what you say from this moment on, I'll know that the only reason you're really here is because of Declan.'

This time it was Louise walking away, heading to the bedroom and pulling out her suitcase. 'You'll hear from my solicitor in a couple of days.'

'Is this what you really want?'

'No,' Louise admitted. 'But I can't do this any more. Maybe I've lived with Maggie too long, maybe I'm chasing that stupid pot of gold at the end of the rainbow, but I want it all, Daniel. I want someone who loves me, someone who's open and honest with me, and no matter how hard you sometimes try, you're simply not prepared to give it.'

'It?'

'It.' Louise nodded. 'Whatever *it* is that keeps holding you back. I watched my parents' marriage fall apart and I'm not going to put Declan through it.'

It took for ever to pack—nappies, toys, bottles, sterilizers. She whizzed through his flat and scrubbed away all the jumble of mess a baby created until it lay in the boot of her car. But the hardest part of all was lifting Declan out of his warm cot and clipping him into the car seat as Daniel watched. 'You can see him on Sunday,' she said firmly, but something died inside as she stepped into the car and finally closed the door, not just on the car but on hope itself.

CHAPTER FOURTEEN

OUTPATIENTS was actually fun.

Well, maybe *fun* was an exaggeration, but despite the gloom in her personal life, Louise found herself enjoying the busy atmosphere: the rapid turnover in the clinics and variety of specialities, along with the chatter and endless stream of patients. For someone whose nerves were rather fraught, the absolute lack of drama was a surprising bonus—any emergency was swiftly dealt with and parcelled off to Emergency!

Though Daniel's name was plastered on many walls and patients' notes, very rarely did he grace the worn carpets of Outpatients, leaving it to his registrar and interns. On the rare occasion he appeared, invariably either Louise found out after the event or was able to avoid him completely.

Though she saw him regularly on the home front.

Twice a week he saw Declan, picking him up from the crèche and bringing him back to her by eight p.m., or for a few hours at the weekend, when he'd arrive at the door and collect his son, along with a nappy bag. But there was no attempt at small talk, no polite conversation or inviting him in.

It was the only way she could survive.

'Amanda!' Louise smiled in happy recognition as she called the name and a familiar face stood up, with a beaming Harry by her side. 'How are you?'

'Fantastic,' Amanda replied, looking nothing like the pale, anxious woman she had seen last. 'I was actually going to go to the surgical ward and see you after this check-up. I've been over a couple of times but you never seemed to be there—now I know why!'

'How's he doing?' Louise asked, as she guided Amanda through to one of the vacant examination rooms and did her observations, writing them down on her notes and placing them on the desk for the registrar who was taking the clinic.

'Really well. He's still upstairs but he's in the nursery now and breathing by himself. He just needs to put on a bit more weight and in a couple of weeks we can take him home.'

'So what did you call him?'

'Harry!' Amanda said shyly, looking up at her very proud husband. 'After his father.'

Luke Evans, the registrar, came in and shook the Bennetts' hands, before running through some questions with Amanda about her post-operative recovery then asking her to lie on the examination couch so he could assess her wound.

'Healing very nicely,' Luke observed. 'We won't need to see you again, Mrs Bennett. A follow-up letter will be sent to your GP, who you should see if you have any concerns, but I don't envisage any problems.'

But as kind and as professional as Luke had been, once he left the room Louise could tell from their slightly downcast faces that they'd been expecting to see Daniel. That was confirmed when Harry pulled out two beautifully wrapped presents.

'We got this for you, Louise,' Amanda said. 'You were wonderful during the labour. I must have given you such a fright.'

'You did,' Louise smiled as she opened a large box of chocolates, able to admit it now that Harry junior was doing so well. 'Thank you so much—that's really thoughtful of you.'

'Is Mr Ashwood around?' Harry asked hopefully, but Louise shook her head.

'His registrar's taking the clinic today,' she answered. 'I'm not actually sure where he is.'

'Well, could you see that he gets this. Please?' Harry offered the other parcel and Louise thanked them on Daniel's behalf. 'We might run into him over the next couple of weeks, given how much time we're spending at the hospital, but just in case we miss him, can you be sure to tell him how grateful we are? To you, too, Louise.' Harry coloured a little bit as he continued, 'And not just for how well you handled the delivery, if you know what I mean.'

'I certainly do!' Louise blushed, too, and not just with embarrassment. Waving them off, as pleased as she was for the Bennetts, their togetherness only exacerbated her own loneliness. The fact she'd been able to help the two of them work things out, and not Daniel and herself.

'Oh, my, look at you!' Any morose feelings were quickly quashed when Louise called her next patient. Expecting a sickly young man to put up his hand for her to wheel him through, or at the very least escort him, Louise was genuinely stunned when six feet of suntanned good looks stood up. And he wasn't alone. A pretty blonde girl fussed over him as he made his way over, and his smile was wide as Louise gaped in admiration. 'You look fantastic!'

'I feel fantastic.' Jordan grinned. He walked with just a slight limp and his speech was only a touch impeded. 'Do you like the hair?'

'Hmm,' Louise grinned at his bleached, waxed spikes.

'This is Ashley.' Jordan couldn't keep the pride out of his voice as he introduced his girlfriend, then gently scolded her. 'I can do this by myself, Ash. Go and get a drink and I'll meet you back here in half an hour or so!'

'How's rehab going?' Louise asked once they were in the examination room.

'OK,' Jordan shrugged, holding out his arm without prompting for his blood pressure to be recorded. 'I had a home assessment last week and I'm supposed to be going home for a trial on Saturday, but the occupational therapist said that if I keep going the way I am, I should be home for good in a couple of weeks.'

'You've done really well!' Louise said warmly, and they weren't empty words. Even with the best medical attention in the world, getting your life back on track after suffering injuries as serious as Jordan's had been came down to sheer grit and determination, of which Jordan clearly had plenty.

'You're going to need to wear a gown because Dr Evans is going to want to have a good look at you…'

'Dr Evans?'

'Dr Evans is taking the clinic this morning,' Louise started to explain, but she was interrupted by the door opening and Daniel appearing with a very wide and very unusual smile— though aimed entirely at his patient.

'I didn't think you were on this morning, Doc.' Jordan grinned.

'I'm supposed to be in a meeting with the radiologist, but

I asked Reception to page me when it was your turn. I wanted to see for myself how you were doing.'

There was genuine warmth and admiration between them that defied age and status. Daniel was clearly delighted by his patient's progress and in turn, despite his tender years, Jordan knew that he'd received far more than just medical care from his doctor.

'Your skin's cleared up nicely,' Daniel observed, 'and the cosmetic surgeons have done some nice work on your facial scarring.' Jordan's care had been more multi-disciplined than most, and he had a list of doctors to see that morning, but Daniel didn't just check his abdomen, he was interested in his entire patient. 'How's the weakness in your arm and leg?'

'Coming along,' Jordan said. 'I'm having a handrail put in the bathroom but, apart from getting in and out of the bath, I can pretty much manage everything—except surfing…'

'Give it time.' Daniel smiled. 'With the progress you've made in last few weeks, if you carry on with the rehab programme and put that bit extra in yourself, I've no doubt in my mind that you'll be back doing what you love in the not-too-distant future.'

'Done any surfing, Doc?' Jordan asked, as Daniel held up a finger and asked him to follow it with his eyes without moving his head.

Louise smothered a smile at the image of the terribly upright Daniel waxing his board and catching a wave.

'None,' Daniel answered. 'Now squeeze my hands as hard as you can.'

'So what sport do you play?' Jordan pressed, lying down when Daniel gestured him to do so and again without prompting lifting each leg in turn as Daniel pressed against his ankle to test the strength in each side. 'Let me guess—cricket?'

'Not any more.' Daniel grimaced, catching Louise's eye as she passed him an ophthalmoscope and even managing to impart a small smile at the memory of his most recent sporting injury.

Finally Daniel examined Jordan's stomach, first reading the reports from the tests Jordan had had earlier in the week and asking how things had been going, then lifting his gown and listening to bowel sounds before gently probing his handiwork.

'Looks like a bit of jigsaw, doesn't it?' Jordan said, nervously making small talk, clearly wanting Daniel to be pleased with his findings—desperate not to have to return to the colostomy bag he had hated so much. 'But I don't mind.'

'It's looking great,' Daniel said. 'I'm very pleased with how things are progressing. But it's very important that if there are problems, you see me sooner rather than later. You've had a lot of surgery on your stomach and there's always a chance that there might be some problems with scar tissue or adhesions. Do you remember me explaining that to you?'

Jordan gave a nod and despite the bravado, despite the spiky hair and piercings, he looked like a nervous teenager who had been through way too much in his short life.

Louise knew how he felt, knew the sadness that had overwhelmed her when there had been a real possibility that Declan might need a colostomy, but also knew that at the end of the day sometimes in life choices had to be faced. As Daniel hesitated for a moment before continuing, Louise knew that he was remembering it, too.

'If there are any problems, I want you to come and see me. Don't put it off because you're worried that you're going to have to have a colostomy. As I've told you many times, that's something we *both* want to avoid.

'Right.' Offering his hand, he helped Jordan to sit up.

'How many more doctors have you got pencilled into your diary today?'

'Just the dermatologist and the psychiatrist.' Jordan rolled his eyes as he got dressed and Louise tidied the room and changed the paper sheet on the examination bed, ready for the next patient. 'Then I'm back next week to see the neurosurgeon.'

'Well, clearly the dermatologist is doing his job.' Daniel smiled. 'And from the smile on your face I'd say you're doing well with the psychiatrist, too.'

'It helps.' Jordan gave a tiny shake of his head, as if he couldn't believe he actually believed it himself. 'You know when you told me I should see a shrink I only agreed to it to get you off my back. But, you know, he's really helped me to make sense of things, deal with all the changes.'

'I'm glad to hear that.'

'You know all my mum kept saying when I first came round was that it didn't matter—that no matter how bad my injuries were, it didn't matter how I looked so long as I was alive. But it did matter to me.' His eyes met Daniel's. 'And you were the only one who seemed to understand that. I didn't want anyone to see me like that, didn't want anyone seeing me at my lowest, and then when Sally dumped me I just kind of hit rock bottom.'

'You clawed your way back, though,' Daniel said. 'And just look at you now.'

'I reckon I've had a lucky escape.' Jordan grinned.

'I'll say. Did you ever see the photos of your car?' But Jordan just laughed.

'I was talking about Sally! I've met someone else—her name's Ashley.' And as he spoke on, Jordan didn't look nineteen all of a sudden. Such was the certainty in his voice it was as if

Jordan was the older, wiser one. 'And I know it's early days, but I also know it's going to work. I thought I was happy with Sally, but now I know I wasn't even close. I know I'd have got through this without Ashley, but it's one hell of a lot easier with her, Doc.'

For the first time the easy chatter between them faltered. Daniel didn't respond straight away, his expression completely unreadable, his eyes a million miles away. But Jordan carried on, not noticing the change in Daniel. 'I've said thanks to all the staff and I've meant it each time, but I owe you a lot more than just thanks, Doc.'

'You owe me nothing.' Daniel's voice was gruff as he snapped back to attention. 'Seeing you doing well is enough reward.'

'Well, I got you this anyway.' Jordan pulled a rather tatty envelope out of his pocket and handed it to him. 'I didn't know what to get you, so I thought of what I'd want.'

Louise was intrigued as Daniel opened the envelope, watched as a smile etched over his face.

'A CD voucher.'

'Yep. Everyone likes music, so I figured you could choose what you liked—wish my bloody aunts would do the same, instead of buying me awful T-shirts and socks all the time.'

'I've got plenty of socks.' Daniel smiled, but his voice was still hoarse. 'Thanks very much, Jordan. It's much appreciated. I'll see you again in another six weeks.'

'I wrote you a message in the card as well…' As Daniel started to open it, Jordan reached out his good hand to stop him. 'Maybe read it later.'

'Come on, Jordan,' Louise said, as Daniel sat down at the desk to write up his findings. 'I'll take you through to the waiting room and let the receptionist know that you're ready for your next appointment.'

After speaking to the receptionist and making sure that Jordan was on the list for the dermatologist, Louise called the next patient in. Elsie Redditch, an elderly lady, needed the varicose ulcers on her ankles to be seen and re-dressed but refused Louise's offer of a wheelchair, proudly insisting on walking but taking for ever to manage the short distance.

'You'll have to shoot me before you put me in one of those things,' she said tartly, but *did* take Louise's arm when she offered it.

'Did you take a painkiller before you came?' Louise asked, hoping that she had as varicose ulcers could be supremely painful.

'Two,' Elsie said, leaning more heavily on Louise's arm as they finally reached the examination room. 'And if they don't work then I'm going to ask them to knock me out next time!'

'We can give you some gas to breathe while we change the dressings if they're really hurting.'

'I'm not in the maternity ward, am I?' Elsie quipped, and Louise grinned at the old lady's sharp wit.

'No, but it's the same sort of gas as is used on the labour ward. You can take as little or as much as you like and it offers temporary relief…' Louise started to explain, but as she opened the examination room her voice trailed off, because sitting at the desk in the examination room where she'd left him maybe fifteen minutes ago was Daniel. His face was in his hands, his back taut with tension as he stared down at the card Jordan had written for him. Despite the chatter, despite the rather abrupt opening of the door, Louise realised he didn't even know anyone was there, lost somewhere in a world of his own.

And if his pain hadn't been so palpable, she'd have just

carried right on in, prompting him to move, but instead she quietly closed the door, affixed the 'engaged' sign then turned to the elderly lady. 'Elsie, I'm sorry to do this, but it would seem this room is already in use. Can I take you to the one next door?'

'Do they have gas in there?' Elsie checked.

'Absolutely.'

She'd sworn that next time he would come to her.

Had sworn never to lay herself open to him again. But that wasn't how love worked. That had been her head talking and now it was her heart.

'Just suck hard on the gas, Elsie,' Louise prompted gently, for despite the urgency in her heart to get to Daniel, she refused to rush the old lady. 'I'm just squirting some saline onto the gauze—it'll feel a bit cold.' She hadn't even started to remove the dressing. A long soak with saline would be needed before she even attempted to remove the dressing, but so painful were these types of ulcers that even a gentle squirt of water could prove agonising.

'Done. How was that?'

'The gas helped,' Elsie said, handing back the mouthpiece and smiling appreciatively at Louise. 'Can I have that when you take them off?'

'Of course,' Louise said. 'Right, are you comfortable there? I'm going to leave them to soak for ten minutes or so and then Dr Evans will be in and we'll remove the dressings.'

Heading out into the corridor, Louise placed the 'engaged' sign and hung Elsie's clipboard on the door to alert Luke he had a patient in there.

'Louise!' May, the charge nurse, paused as she dashed past. 'Do you want to go to coffee?'

'Please,' Louise answered. 'I'm soaking some varicose ulcer dressings in exam 4, a seventy-eight-year-old lady named Elsie Redditch. I've laid everything out for Dr Evans. They're very painful. She needed gas—'

'Fine,' May interrupted, more than used to re-dressing ulcers, but smiling to Louise for bringing her up to speed. 'How are you enjoying Outpatients?'

'A lot,' Louise answered honestly.

'Not quite the drama of a busy surgical ward.' May smiled. 'But we still know how to keep you busy. You know, I've been very pleased with your work. There's a permanent job coming up after Christmas—maybe you should think about applying for it. Preference is given to internal applicants. And,' she added, calling over her shoulder as she bustled off, 'the hours are great for a busy working mum.'

Which was what she was, Louise realised. A busy working mum, who might not be blazing a trail in her career, might not be earning her stripes on a high-dependency surgical unit, but there would be time for all that later. Right now she was making a living, using her brain and keeping busy, and Louise realised with a shiver of pride at being offered a permanent job—she *was* doing OK.

Unlike Daniel.

Gently opening the door, completely unsure of his reaction, she tiptoed in to see he was still where she left him, only this time he turned around a touch when she came in. His face was such a picture of abject misery that she ignored her head and followed her heart. She crossed the room and placed her hand on his shoulder, feeling the tension beneath her fingers, half ex-

pecting him to shrug her off or ask her to leave—bracing herself
for another rejection—never envisaging what would come next.

Instead of pushing her away, he was pulling her towards him,
gathering her to him, holding her, pulling her onto his lap, rough
with need. His desperate mouth found hers, pressing his lips to
hers, parting them with his tongue, kissing her as if he was
drawing from her, his arms wrapped so tightly around her she
could barely breathe. But she didn't need air, just needed him,
drew from him, absorbed him. And it was so completely out of
character, this formal, conscientious man caressing her at work,
his rough hands searching her body, his face scratching hers, his
kiss so rough and demanding, so desperate and hungry, his
emotions so out of control in this tiny, closed room, that sensi-
bility might have dictated fear and yet all she felt was him.

Knew that in his own way this was Daniel coming to her,
perhaps for the first time, asking without words for help to
get through. And it wasn't an apology this time, Louise knew
that, but a plea for understanding—a need, a desire to escape
whatever it was that haunted him. And she allowed him that
temporary reprieve—let him draw on her for comfort.

So she kissed him back, felt the hard, lean lines of his
body pressed against her, kissed him back with the fierce
passion he clearly needed, obliterated his pain for as long as
she could—empowered by his desire. Because even if he
hadn't said a word, for the very first time he wasn't holding
back. Even if he wasn't telling her what she needed to know,
Louise knew it would come, knew by his frenzied kiss, his
disregard for protocol, his utter, blatant want, that finally he
was giving that little piece of him she'd so desperately craved.

Eventually he pulled back before it could go any further,
before the urge to take her there and then became too over-

whelming. He released her just enough to look into her eyes, and it was all there. Even if he hadn't said a word, everything she really needed to know was there.

'He wrote that he's actually glad in some ways that it happened.' There were tears in his dark eyes as Daniel handed her the card and she silently read it. 'Glad for what he went through. How can he be?'

'Because he's come out the other side,' Louise ventured, trying and praying that she'd say the right thing. 'Because he's happier now than he was before the accident.'

'I'll never be glad that *it* happened.'

And as he offered her the elusive *it*, she touched his damp cheek and gently shook her head.

'You don't have to tell me.'

She actually meant it—her thirst for more intimate knowledge quenched now. Quite simply, she loved him, trusted him enough now, to spare him the unnecessary pain of reliving it if he truly didn't want to, the kiss they had just shared telling her way more than words ever could have.

'I had AML.' He ignored her offer, starting perhaps at the hardest part. AML, short for acute myeloid leukaemia, was a devastating illness that struck the young and was one of the most fatal of the leukaemias. Even without hearing the rest, she closed her eyes for a second, knowing that he would have been through hell. 'I had everything going for me. I was in my final year at med school, on the first rugby and cricket teams, and I was in love…' He frowned for a second, asking with his eyes if it was OK to say that, and she nodded, nodded because somehow she'd known he must have been. 'Her name was Kate, she was in the same year as me, and we just knew we were going to be together. You know how you just know?'

Again she nodded, because the second she'd laid eyes on him that had been exactly how she'd felt. 'Kate got pregnant—a complete accident but, you know, I was pleased. We both worked it all out—she'd take a year off and then pick up her career. We were going to make it…' And though it hurt like hell to hear about her, to know that he'd truly loved before, it was far less painful than being denied his past, so Louise listened, listened as he told her how much he'd loved and how his whole world had fallen apart.

'I started coming out in bruises and I was tired all the time. I tried to put it down to working and playing too hard. I was working in a bar some nights, trying to save up for the baby, and I decided that the bruises were from a rough game at the weekend, but in a matter of days I knew I was in real trouble. I went and had a blood test one lunchtime and by the evening I was lying in a bed in the oncology ward, booked in for a bone-marrow biopsy in the morning and asking Kate to bring in my oncology textbooks.

'The more the results came in, the worse it looked. The prognosis was awful and I knew that even if I did make it through, the next year or two were just going to be an endless round of chemo and hospital. But my family were great, I had amazing friends and I had Kate and the baby…' His face screwed up as if he was right back there, living it all over again, so instead of looking at him she held him, buried her face in his shoulders, felt his face in her hair, his body dragging in air as he steadied himself.

'The day the chemo started I had to sign all the forms, was told that I'd undoubtedly be left infertile, that if I'd been well enough to I could have left samples for the future. But I was really ill by then—I mean, really ill—so they just went ahead with the treatment. Kate didn't come by for a few days and if I'm honest, I was just too out of it to really notice. But when she did…' He wasn't holding her now, it was Louise holding him, waiting patiently for whatever came next. And when he couldn't go on, she tried to make it easier for him, said words that must hurt so much to speak out loud.

'She'd lost the baby,' Louise said softly, and it wasn't a question but a statement, so sure she had been that she now understood his pain, never having fathomed how deep it really ran.

'She'd ended the pregnancy.'

Louise felt her heart stop for a moment, all the platitudes she'd been silently rehearsing since he'd first started to tell her imploding—because nothing she could say could make this right. 'Without discussing it with you?'

'She probably knew I'd try to talk her out of it.' Louise sat on his lap and stared aghast at him, all her training flying out of the window—staying impassive an impossible feat when it was someone you loved in pain.

'I tried not to blame her—I mean, I was so wrapped up in myself I never stopped to think how scared she must have been, knowing that I was probably going to die and that even if I lived, effectively she'd be coping on her own for a while. Money would have been tight—'

'No!' Angrily Louise shook her head. 'They're all just excuses, Daniel, and you know it. And I'm not talking about whether Kate was right or wrong to end the pregnancy—I'd never, ever judge—but to make that decision for you, to take away your chance of fatherhood without even discussing it with you…'

Tears filled her eyes as she heard her own words, the ramifications of what she'd done to him hitting home again. 'I'm sorry,' she gasped, salty, stinging tears rolling down her cheeks. 'I'm so, so sorry that I did it to you again…'

'Louise!' His voice was firm, hands holding her shoulders, forcing her to face him, and when that didn't work he shook her gently, until finally she dared. 'Don't ever compare yourself to her. *You* gave me a son, you gave me a child I never thought I could have…'

'But I didn't tell you.'

'And now I understand why.' She could hear the strength back in his voice now, the strong, resilient man she adored back now, steadying her, soothing her, *understanding* her. 'All you ever did was try to love me, and all I ever did was push you away. I swore, the day I found out what Kate had done, that I'd never let anyone close again. I was the only one on that ward who welcomed isolation, welcomed the chance to shut the world out—but I know that I was wrong. That's why I spent time with Jordan. I could see him doing what I had—and I didn't want him living the life that follows.

'You were the best thing that ever happened to me, Louise. The day you walked over to do that ward round in London, smiled that dizzy smile—I fell in love, even though I didn't want to.'

Which was a whole lot better than adore—a whole lot—and if she hadn't been crying so hard she'd have stopped him right there, made him say it all over again. But instead she listened, listened as this beautiful, complicated man told her what was in his heart.

'And it terrified me,' Daniel admitted. 'Terrified me, because I hadn't felt that way in more than a decade, had sworn I'd never *allow* myself to feel that way again. So I ended it, even kidded myself that I was doing you a favour, that you deserved someone who could give you a baby—but the truth was I just didn't want to get hurt again.'

'I'd never have hurt you...' Louise gulped.

'I took care of that myself,' Daniel said softly. 'I soon realised what a stupid mistake I'd made so I came to Australia, thought I'd get myself a job and get settled and then I'd look you up. But I just couldn't do that last bit. I knew that if I told you how much you meant to me...'

'You really came here for me?'

'It's the *only* reason I'm here, Louise.'

And he said it so firmly she knew it was the absolute truth. Reeling inside that this man she had thought so barren of emotion would follow her to the other side of the world. That he *loved* her enough to give it all up and follow his heart. If he'd stopped talking there and then, it would have been enough, for not a single doubt shadowed her mind now. But he was making up for so much lost time, revealing not just to her but himself the true depth of his emotions...

And she loved him even more for it.

'When I found out you had a baby, I was disappointed, angry even. Hell, I hadn't expected you to go into a life of seclusion, but after what we had together I thought you'd need some time—but it still didn't stop the way I was feeling. The night I came to the flat I was really hoping we could sort things out—had even kidded myself that maybe it was for the best. If I couldn't give you a child, then...'

'You really would have taken Declan on, even if he wasn't yours?'

'I don't know,' he admitted softly. 'But I was prepared to

try. I just couldn't stand the thought of you lying to me, telling me he was mine when I knew…'

'You knew nothing,' Louise said softly. 'You knew nothing about how I felt about you. Daniel, there could never have been anyone else—a year on and I was *still* trying to get over you, and failing spectacularly!'

'That morning when you were feeding him…' he looked at her as if she should know the one he meant, but Louise gave a bemused frown.

'I feed him every morning.'

'That last morning,' he said. 'You'd had a full night's sleep and you said you felt wonderful. You *looked* wonderful, Louise, you *were* wonderful, and I hated myself because I still couldn't tell you what I was really feeling, still couldn't even admit it to myself.'

'So,' she said slowly, 'what are you feeling now?'

'That I can't do this for a moment longer. I love you, Louise, and I can't fight with you over a baby we both love, too. And I can't blame you for all my mistakes.'

'But can you forgive me for mine?' Louise asked, because it was important, because she couldn't live the rest of her life defending herself, but as Daniel answered her with a kiss, she soon realised that neither could he.

'Marry me,' Daniel said, much, much later, when his pager was screaming in his pocket and Louise was trying to work out an excuse for an extremely prolonged coffee-break! 'Tomorrow.'

'It's not that easy.' Louise grinned, and she didn't even need to qualify it, didn't need to explain to him she was question-ing the date, not the fact they would be together.

'Why not?' Daniel grumbled.

'I think you need a licence or something.' Louise giggled. 'And given that you're only here on holiday…'

'Hmm,' Daniel said, clearly trying to work his way around the problem.

'I have to get back,' Louise said reluctantly. 'How on earth am I going to explain to May where I've been? She just offered me a permanent job and this is how I repay her!'

'Tell her that Mr Ashwood just proposed to you,' Daniel grinned

'Well, it would be the perfect excuse.' Louise laughed, knowing she'd never do it in a million years. Her hand was on the door as she reluctantly headed back to work, but it was too late because May was already opening it, flustered and more than a little annoyed.

'Where on earth have you been, Louise? Oh.' Momentarily she faltered. 'Hello, Mr Ashwood. Sorry, Louise, I didn't realise you were already back from your break!'

'Actually, she's not.' Daniel smiled at the elderly sister. 'It's entirely my fault she's late back, May. You see…'

Louise's mouth gaped open. She truly thought he had been joking, couldn't believe that Daniel was going to share this happy news, couldn't believe the smile on that usually impassive face. And clearly neither could May because she was frowning at the change in the usually distant consultant. 'I was just proposing to her.'

'Proposing what exactly?' May asked dubiously, her eyes swivelling from Daniel to Louise and then back to Daniel.

'Marriage!' Daniel beamed and May started to smile, too.

'And did she give you a reply?'

'Actually, now you mention it, no, she didn't.'

'Two minutes,' May said sternly, as she looked over at

Louise, but her eyes were smiling. 'And you can make up the time during your lunch-break!'

Alone again with him, she smiled shyly.

'Yes, please.'

'When?' Daniel asked. 'I'm not going to give you a moment to change your mind. We'll just have to sort out the immigration and stuff!'

Louise had the perfect answer.

'I know the name of a very good solicitor,' she said, coming over and whispering into his ear, imagining the look on Ms Corporate Suit's face when they strolled into her office hand in hand.

As a family.

EPILOGUE

'DID you know that at some of the London hospitals, if it's your second baby, you get a free tummy tuck!'

They were thirty thousand feet in the air, the three of them snuggled in the leather seats of business class, courtesy of the fact she was six months pregnant and on their way to a whole new life.

How dare he try to sleep?

'I must have missed that article in the *BMJ*,' Daniel drawled, pulling up his eyeshields and taking the glossy magazine she was reading. After flicking on his reading light and skimming through the article she had slowly devoured, he said, 'She had a Caesarean.'

'I might have to have one.' Louise beamed hopefully. 'And given you're a consultant there, maybe they'll give me a freebie, too.'

'Louise,' Daniel said patiently, 'they don't give free tummy tucks, and even if they did, why on earth do you think that you'd need one?'

'I don't *need* one.' Louise shrugged. 'But if I *did* have to have a Caesarean and the surgeon offered—'

'Which he wouldn't,' Daniel interrupted.

'Well, if he does, remember to say yes for me,' Louise mumbled, as he pulled down his eyeshields and, because he was male, managed to fall asleep in a matter of seconds.

Or so she thought.

'I promise,' Daniel said solemnly a few moments later, pulling off his eyeshields and tossing them over his shoulder, giving up on the only chance of sleep he'd had in the last twenty-four hours, 'that *if* you have a Caesarean, and *if* Greg Harrison offers a quick nip and tuck at the same time, I'll sign the form on your behalf!'

'Thank you.' Louise smiled, not because he'd agreed but because he'd taken his eyeshields off, because he understood that she needed him now.

'What's wrong?'

'Nothing,' Louise answered, but Daniel gave her a very disbelieving frown.

'Are you worried about missing your family?'

'Heavens, no.' She rolled her eyes. 'In fact, from the way they're talking about coming over to visit, I think I'm going to be seeing more of them living in London than I did when I was in Melbourne.'

'You know a lot of people in London,' Daniel reminded her, in case that was what was on her mind. 'And Maggie might be back in a few months.'

'I know.' Louise nodded but she knew he was waiting for her to elaborate, knew that the silence between them would have to be filled soon.

Because that was how it was now—no holding back, no letting problems fester. All the love and honesty she'd always craved surrounded her now. The Daniel she had always known had been there was beside her now, and she was never going to let him slip back to his old ways—never going to let him shut her out for even a moment—and, therefore, Louise knew that neither, then, must she.

'So what's wrong?' Daniel pushed, breaking into her thoughts. 'And don't say "Nothing" again.'

'But that's the problem!' Louise answered cryptically. 'Nothing! I haven't got a single thing to worry about. I can't wait to start our new life in London, Declan's growing more gorgeous every minute, and I just know the baby's going to be fine…' She watched as his hand moved across and tenderly stroked her ripe stomach. 'Everyone says that second labours are easy-peasy and I know this time I'll have you with me. It's just…'

'Just what, Louise?'

She blurted it out, just blurted it out, half expecting him to laugh, half expecting him to put his eyeshields on and go back to sleep. 'I just can't get used to feeling this happy.'

He didn't laugh, didn't even smile, just nodded his under-standing.

'Sometimes I wake up in the night and think that surely it can't last…'

'Don't you think we've had our share of problems?' Daniel asked. 'That maybe we both deserve to feel like this for a while?'

'That's just it,' Louise answered. 'Now I'm worrying about when the bubble will burst.'

'How about never?' Daniel offered, but Louise shook her head, sure that it couldn't be that easy. 'OK how about I promise that I'm going to spend the rest of my life making sure the bubble stays intact?'

'And if it doesn't?' Louise asked. 'They're very fragile, you know!'

'Then I'll blow us another one,' Daniel said assuredly. 'Because nothing's going to come between us, Louise, and I reckon that together we can deal with just about anything. Which means just one thing…'

Reaching out for her in the dimmed cabin, her kissed her softly. 'You, Mrs Ashwood, are just going to have to get used to being happy!'

MILLS & BOON®   0107/03b

Live the emotion

Medical
romance™

THE LONDON CONSULTANT'S RESCUE
by Joanna Neil

Dr Emma Granger enjoys rescuing people all over
London with the air ambulance team. Her boss, Rhys
Benton, is professional, caring and fully in control
– everything a consultant should be. Emma believes
that he could never see her as anything more than
a colleague, but when Emma's life is in danger, Rhys
has the opportunity to show her how he really feels.

THE DOCTOR'S BABY SURPRISE
by Gill Sanderson

Gorgeous doctor Toby Sinclair has a reputation as
a carefree playboy. But when his baby son – who he
never knew existed – lands on his doorstep,
Dr Annie Arnold can't refuse Toby's plea for help.
And as Annie watches Toby bonding with his baby,
she wonders if they might just have a future together
after all…

THE SPANISH DOCTOR'S CONVENIENT
BRIDE *by Meredith Webber*

Obstetrician Marty Cox cannot help growing
attached to the baby girl in NICU, but she knows
that the father – when they find him – will want to
take his child away. The attraction between Marty
and Dr Carlos Quintero is instant and, realising how
devoted Marty is to his daughter, Carlos proposes a
marriage of convenience.

On sale 2nd February 2007

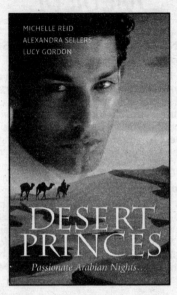

DL

4 FREE

BOOKS AND A SURPRISE GIFT!

We would like to take this opportunity to thank you for reading this Mills & Boon® book by offering you the chance to take FOUR more specially selected titles from the Medical Romance™ series absolutely FREE! We're also making this offer to introduce you to the benefits of the Mills & Boon® Reader Service™—

- ★ **FREE home delivery**
- ★ **FREE gifts and competitions**
- ★ **FREE monthly Newsletter**
- ★ **Exclusive Reader Service offers**
- ★ **Books available before they're in the shops**

Accepting these FREE books and gift places you under no obligation to buy, you may cancel at any time, even after receiving your free shipment. Simply complete your details below and return the entire page to the address below. You don't even need a stamp!

YES! Please send me 4 free Medical Romance books and a surprise gift. I understand that unless you hear from me, I will receive 6 superb new titles every month for just £2.80 each, postage and packing free. I am under no obligation to purchase any books and may cancel my subscription at any time. The free books and gift will be mine to keep in any case.

M7ZED

Ms/Mrs/Miss/Mr ....Initials ....
                                                                                BLOCK CAPITALS PLEASE
Surname ....
Address ....
....
....Postcode................................

Send this whole page to:
UK: FREEPOST CN8I, Croydon, CR9 3WZ